how to

steal a car

PETE HAUTMAN

SCHOLASTIC INC.
New York Toronto London Auckland
Sydney Mexico City New Delhi Hong Kong

No part of this publication may be reproduced, stored in a retrieval system, or transmitted in any form or by any means, electronic, mechanical, photocopying, recording, or otherwise, without written permission of the publisher. For information regarding permission, write to Scholastic Inc., Attention: Permissions Department, 557 Broadway, New York, NY 10012.

This book was originally published in hardcover by Scholastic Press in 2009.

ISBN 978-0-545-11287-1

12 11 10 9 8 7 6 5 4 3 2 1   11 12 13 14 15 16/0

Printed in the U.S.A.   40
First paperback printing, January 2011

The text type was set in Adobe Caslon Pro.
Book design by Christopher Stengel

For Maddie Shae

Whenever I find myself growing grim about the mouth; whenever it is a damp, drizzly November in my soul; whenever I find myself involuntarily pausing before coffin warehouses, and bringing up the rear of every funeral I meet . . . it requires a strong moral principle to prevent me from deliberately stepping into the street, and methodically knocking people's hats off — then, I account it high time to get to sea as soon as I can. This is my substitute for pistol and ball.

— from the first paragraph of *Moby-Dick* by Herman Melville

The way this whole thing got started was completely coincidental and not like I planned it or anything. Jen and I had been at Ridgedale a few days before and we got kicked out of Abercrombie & Fitch because Jen was carrying around this enormous drippy waffle cone, so we went outside and sat on one of the benches in front of Macy's so she could suck down the rest of it. We were talking and watching people walk to and from their cars when I noticed this salesman-type guy younger than our parents but way older than us score a prize parking slot close to the front entrance. The guy got out looking very pleased with himself and set his car keys on the hood and started digging in his briefcase for something. His keys slid off the hood and landed by his feet. He didn't notice.

I looked at Jen but she was having some sort of crisis with her cone.

A couple seconds later, the guy found whatever it was he was looking for. He closed his briefcase and took off toward the Macy's entrance, passing real close to us. I opened my mouth to tell him he'd dropped his keys, but for some reason I didn't. After he was gone I said to Jen, "That guy dropped his keys."

"Where?"

I walked over to his car and picked them up. I don't remember what kind of car it was — something boring, a Toyota or Honda or something. When I got back to the bench, Jen was staring at the last inch of her waffle cone with this tragic expression on her face.

"I didn't get a malted milk ball in the bottom," she said.

"I don't think Flavor Hut does the milk ball thing. You have to go to Cold Stone for that."

"That sucks."

It did suck, no malted milk ball, but what could you do? Jen walked the soggy tip of her cone over to the cans on the other side of the entrance and tossed it into the recycling.

"Wrong can," I said.

She shrugged and wiped her fingers on her butt. "We better go find him," she said.

"Find who?"

"The key guy."

"I'm sure he's got another set," I said, putting the keys in my purse.

Jen looked at me like I was this psycho, but she was the one who just threw her ice cream cone in the recycling can, so I ignored her.

"Let's go back to Abercrombie," I said. "I want to try on that top with the rhinestones."

"You know you'll never buy it. It actually might look good on you." Jen had some very definite opinions on my fashion sense. She thought I dressed like a nun, which was not completely untrue.

"You never know," I said. "Maybe today I'll have an aneurysm and buy something pink and sparkly."

The week before, Jen and I had been at the Minnehaha Club pool and Jen was giving me grief about my swimsuit.

"You should get a two-piece," she told me. "You'd look hot."

"Are you saying I don't look hot now?" I was wearing a black one-piece, skimpier than a nun would wear — if nuns ever went swimming.

"No! I just think you'd look hotter in a bikini. You're so conservative."

So of course I immediately felt like the boringest person on earth — but I didn't say anything, even though it bugged me.

A little while later we were ogling these two guys, maybe eighteen or nineteen, and Jen said, "I'll take the blond."

"Fine. I'll settle for the one with the six-pack abs."

"Damien."

"Damien?"

"He looks like a Damien. And the other one looks like a Troy."

"Not Troy. Andre."

"Okay, Andre. Damien and Andre."

We were laughing — okay, giggling — and sipping our iced teas and absorbing megawatts of cancer-causing UV rays. We were also bored out of our minds, so I decided I'd walk over to Damien and Andre and say something because it was the last thing Jen would ever expect Boring Conservative Me to do. I figured I'd never see them again, and they were too old for us anyway, so what did I have to lose? I stood up and walked over, imagining Jen's eyes wide on my back.

Up close they weren't nearly as good-looking as I'd thought. The blond one had little bumps all over his face like old acne, and the one with the six-pack abs had kind of squished-together features, like the space between his eyes could have used another half inch.

I said, mostly to the one with the squished features and the abs, "So, are you guys members here?"

They looked a little startled. Then their eyes went up and down my body the way guys' eyes do. My suit might have been the most boring conservative bathing suit at the pool, but the way those guys looked at me, it might as well have been Saran Wrap.

I said, "Because if you're not members, I probably shouldn't be talking to you." Where that came from, I had no idea. I wasn't even a member myself — Jen's parents were.

The blond one — Damien or Andre, I'd already forgotten which was which — said, "You're already talking to us."

"Then you must be members."

"I guess so," said Damien. Or Andre.

I wasn't sure what to say next, so I just smiled and shrugged.

"So . . . what's happening?" said the blond.

"Nothing — just another boring day at the country club." I pointed at Jen, who was watching openmouthed from forty feet away. "My friend says you guys are named Damien and Andre. But I forget which of you is which."

They looked at each other and laughed.

"Why don't you invite your friend over here?" said the blond.

I waved Jen over. She looked behind her, like I was waving at someone else. I waved harder. She got up and came toward us, slowly, giving them plenty of time to check her out.

What Jen looks like: same height as me, straight hair that gets streaky blond in the summer but goes to honey brown in the winter, blue eyes, a nose and chin that are both a little longer and pointier than she'd like, and the body of a gymnast, which makes sense, because she *was* a gymnast before she blew out her left knee. She doesn't limp or anything but her doctor told her no more floor exercises or dismounts, so she kind of gave up on the whole Olympics thing. But she still has the hot body, which, as far as most guys are concerned, makes up for any excess facial pointiness. She makes the most of it by wearing the skimpiest swimsuits permitted at the Minnehaha Club. Thongs are forbidden — this is Minnesota, after all — but it would still take five or six of her suits to add up to as much fabric as mine.

By the time Jen arrived, Damien and Andre had done that wordless guy thing where they put dibs on who gets who. The blond was all over Jen, which was fine with me. It took him about ten seconds to tell her how hot she was and that he was a student at the U and that they were going to this great party later and would we like to come. My guy, whose actual name turned out to be Tyler, tried to impress me by telling me he drove a BMW. I told him my name was Cordelia — which it isn't. From there the conversation just kept getting stupider. I mean, any college guy who wants to date a fifteen-year-old is a total loser as far as I'm concerned, but they were kind of fun to talk to, so we hung out with them for an hour or so, then told them we had to go home and get dressed for the "great party" they were taking us to. We said we'd meet them at eight o'clock at the Starbucks on Winnetka.

"I can't believe you did that," Jen said after we left the pool.

"Neither can I," I said. I loved the way she was looking at me, all amazed. So much for boring and conservative.

That night at eight, Jen and I were at the Starbucks on Winnetka. Not like we would actually go to a party with those guys. But we were curious to see if they'd show up.

They never did.

Back to the car keys thing. I figured I'd hang on to them for a souvenir. I liked the idea of having a set of car keys in my purse, and that's probably all that would have happened except that a week later I found out where the key guy lived.

I was with my mom in her Toyota Camry, driving her to Book Club, which was an unutterably boring way to spend two hours, but it was a chance to get in some driving practice and I had homework to do. I'd gotten my permit, and I'd passed the written test, so it was legal for me to drive as long as I had an over-twenty-one adult in the passenger seat. The problem was, my parents hardly ever let me drive at all because my dad did not "passenger well" and my mom always had some excuse, like she was in a huge hurry and didn't want me to get a speeding ticket before I even had a license. Book Club was an opportunity because this was the sort of book club where half the women don't even bother to read the book and they each toss back like six glasses of chardonnay apiece and spend more time dishing than book-talking. My mom would have a serious DUI-worthy buzz going by the time things broke up, and I was the designated driver because the law doesn't say anything about the over-twenty-one person being sober. So I drove her to Betsy Charlesworth's. Betsy has a huge house and no kids, perfect for Book Club. I grabbed a brownie and some little cookies from the sideboard and planted myself on the periphery of the group to read my summer novel, the incredibly thick *Moby-Dick*, while tuning in now and then on the juicier bits of gossip. I think I ended up reading about ten pages. It was actually quite funny in places. The book, I mean.

It was on our way home, with my mom chatting boozily about Ginny Ahlstrand's sudden suspicious weight loss and the declining quality of Betsy Charlesworth's deviled eggs, that I saw the key guy. I probably wouldn't have recognized him except that he happened to be getting out of his familiar-looking car with the same familiar-looking briefcase and he had the same hurried look I remembered from before. He was only like five blocks away from our house, which I guess makes him a neighbor.

You see what I mean about coincidental.

"Turn here," my mom said.

"I've only lived in this neighborhood my whole entire life," I said.

"You're fifteen years old."

I gave her a look. "I can count."

"Are you going to tell me how many glasses of wine I had?"

"No."

"Good. Don't mention it to your father, either."

That night — I don't know why, but I remember it was a Thursday — I called Jen and made her promise to meet me at Burger King at midnight. It took some convincing, because the BK was almost a mile from her house, but I told her I had this secret and if she ever wanted to know what it was she had to show up. In the end she said okay, and after we hung up I started working on homework, never mind that tenth grade didn't even start until September. The American educational system gone berserk. Not only did I have to read a "classic novel" from a list they gave us and report on it (I'd never have picked *Moby-Dick* if I'd known how long it was), I also had to write a five-hundred-word essay of "acceptable quality" on how to do something. How to Tie a Shoe. How to Apply Lip Gloss. How to Become a Vampire. How to Build a Spaceship. How to Write a Five-Hundred-Word Essay. All for an extra half point added to my language arts grade. Woo-hoo.

I worked for like half an hour and only got thirty-five words written. Four hundred sixty-five to go. Good thing I still had a couple months to work on it.

I got to the BK first and bought some fries. Jen took forever to get there. I was sitting at one of the outside tables, fishing little crumbles of french fry from the bottom of the bag and thinking about all the times Jen had disappointed me, like the time we were supposed to go to camp together and she backed out at the last second, leaving me friendless and bored for two weeks at Camp Wannamakemepuke or whatever.

Finally she showed up.

"You're late," I said.

"Look at you," she said, looking at me.

"What?"

She sat down. "All ninja."

I was wearing my black Pilates tights and a black cotton hoodie.

"Not too 'conservative' for you?" I stood up and pulled the hood over my head.

"So what's the big secret?"

"C'mon." I grabbed her hand and pulled her up.

"I don't get to eat?"

"Later."

She complained practically the whole way, all whiny because I wouldn't tell her what we were doing. I *shhh*ed her as we approached the house, staying close to a row of lilac bushes. We were in luck. I'd been afraid the guy would put his car in the garage, but there it was, parked in his driveway.

"Wait here," I said.

How I usually dress: like an off-duty nun, just like Jen says. No one on earth owns more black and gray. If you saw me on TV you might think I was out of some old black-and-white movie. My idea of festive is black pants with a gray blouse. Even my mother thinks I lack fashion sense. "You should wear something fun," she has said on many occasions, often upon presenting me with something "fun," like a multi-colored polka-dot shirt, or a pair of "designer" jeans with carefully applied rips, or striped socks, or red shoes. Yes, she actually bought me a pair of red shoes.

I do not wear red shoes or striped socks. I do not wear blue jeans or any other color of denim. I don't want to look like every other girl. I don't want people to judge me by my clothes. I have other reasons too. My dad actually gets me on this. He dresses kind of the same way, only he wears white shirts, which I never do. I like to shop, though, and when Jen and I get into it at the mall, I'll try on *anything*, the more colorful and bizarre the better. But not in the real world. It drives Jen crazy. And my mom.

———

How to Steal a Car
by
Kelleigh Monahan

When nobody is looking you sneak up to the car and get in and start it. Then drive away. That's pretty much all there is to it.

———

I unlocked the driver's door, slipped behind the wheel, put the key in the ignition, and turned it. The car started right away. I waved at Jen to get in. She shook her head and pressed her body back into the lilac bushes. I put the car in gear and backed out of the driveway. I drove around the block. When I got back to the driveway, Jen had left the shelter of the bushes and was walking quickly down the sidewalk toward home. I pulled up alongside her and rolled down the passenger window.

"Need a lift?" My voice sounded weird and my heart was banging around like a munchkin in a mosh pit.

Jen stuck her head in the window and said in a loud whisper, "What are you *doing*?"

"Going for a ride," I said.

"Are you *crazy*?"

"Maybe. Get in."

I didn't think she was going to do it, but then she opened the passenger door and hopped inside. Her cheeks were flushed. I knew her heart had to be banging like crazy too.

"Go!" she said. "Go! Go!"

We went.

I did not have this screwed-up home life that you would think would drive me to crime. My parents were nearly perfect. I don't mean *perfect* perfect, but compared to a lot of parents, like the ones who beat their kids and lock them in closets and smoke crack and stuff, my parents were practically ideal. For one thing, they were still married after twenty years, and they were completely nonviolent, and neither of them had ever been arrested as far as I know. My dad was a lawyer who ran three miles every morning except Sunday, when he worked as a deacon at our church. He'd been doing that ever since I could remember. My mom worked part-time selling real estate and belonged to like a dozen different do-good organizations — PTA, MADD, ASPCA, AAA — I don't know what all else. And no, she was not a drunk. Only at Book Club. And sometimes wedding receptions. Other than that, she was almost perfect, and even when she wasn't, she tried really hard.

I remember one time when she came rushing home at like ten minutes to six with a bag from Byerly's. I was sitting at the kitchen table doing some lame American history assignment. She pulled a slab of deli lasagna out of the Byerly's bag, fitted it into a pan, and stuck it in the oven. She had also bought some corn salad and roasted peppers. She said nothing to me as she transferred the salad and peppers from their plastic cartons into a matching set of serving bowls.

I said, "Wow."

My mother stopped what she was doing and looked directly at me for the first time. She winked at me, which she never does, then went back into action, stashing the Byerly's cartons in the trash and opening a bottle of wine and making up a bread basket with some organic dinner rolls, also from Byerly's.

Twenty minutes later my dad got home and we sat down to eat. We always ate dinner together, because my nearly perfect mother had once read an article that said children thrived in families that ate home-cooked meals together every night.

"Great lasagna," my dad said.

"Thank you," said my mother.

"New recipe?"

"I just tweaked it a little," she said, then winked at me — again.

I remember now. It was a Nissan Altima. I don't know what color.

I drove fast out of Golden Valley and got on the freeway heading north. Jen and I were both talking at the same time, neither of us really saying anything, just blowing off this wild energy. There was a lot of "Omigod, omigod, I can't believe we're doing this" and Jen talking about all the people who were going to totally freak when they heard about it. Finally I sort of calmed down and said, "We can't tell anybody."

Jen looked stricken.

"I'm serious," I said. "If we tell anybody at all, it might get back to our parents. Or the police."

Jen nodded, then said, "Not even Will?"

Will was our boyfriend, sort of.

"We can tell Will," I said. "He doesn't talk." That wasn't true, exactly. Will Ford spoke perfectly well — he just didn't do it often, which was probably why we were friends. He was the perfect listener. If you told him something and said it was a secret, you couldn't even get him to tell it back to you.

Jen nodded and smiled. As long as she could tell at least one person, she was fine.

"Where should we go?" I asked.

"I don't know," Jen said. "It's after midnight. It's a weekday."

We were almost out of the suburbs, about twenty miles north of Minneapolis, with new housing developments and the remnants of farms on either side of us. I saw some lights up ahead on the right. A low building surrounded by SUVs and pickup trucks came into sight. The neon sign on the roof read B.J.'s BUNKHOUSE, LIVE NUDE DANCERS 24 HOURS.

"Want to stop off for a beer?" I said.

Jen laughed — but she stopped when I turned onto the exit ramp.

"Hey . . . ," she said, sitting forward.

"I'm just turning around," I told her.

She slumped back in her seat saying nothing as I turned away from B.J. and his Live Nude Dancers, crossed under the freeway, and turned onto the southbound entrance ramp.

"We could hit the twenty-four-hour Taco Bell," I said.

"Okay." I could tell the thrill was wearing off for her. I could feel it in myself too. The fun part of stealing a car is pretty short-lived if you have no place to go.

The Taco Bell was close to home and I thought maybe we'd run into somebody we knew, but we didn't — we just ate some really disgusting thing with way too much cheese in it. Then I dropped Jen off at her house, parked the car a block from the key guy's house, and walked home.

I kept the keys.

When I got home, a text from Jen was waiting.

OMG I CAN'T BELIEVE WE DID THAT! she wrote.

I couldn't believe it either.

My father is enormous. As far as I know he has never hit anybody, but he looks like a guy who would. He's about six-five with these huge shoulders and when he wears a shirt with an open collar you can see the mat of gorilla hair covering his chest. And he has big thick eyebrows and dark eyes, and hands so big he can pick up a basketball the way a normal person grabs a softball.

Of course he knows how he looks. He laughs about it. He says it comes in handy in court. My dad practices criminal law, which means he defends all sorts of scumbags, and he says being so big helps him intimidate witnesses. I guess he sort of leans over them and exudes waves of testosterone until they crack.

I just thank God I didn't inherit his enormousness or his hairiness.

It was around the time Jen and I stole the Nissan that my dad got involved with Elwin Carl Dandridge, the serial rapist. Elwin Carl Dandridge was a skinny little guy, half white, half black, and half something else — gray, maybe — who specialized in terrorizing college students over at the U. He raped eight girls in two months before they caught him. As far as the police were concerned, it was a no-brainer. They had DNA and everything, but because it was what my dad calls an "above-the-fold-headline case," he offered to represent Dandridge pro bono (that means for free), even though he had to know that Dandridge was guilty, which was pretty embarrassing for me, because nobody wants their dad to be a rapist-defender.

"Look, it's not like he's going to get off," I told Jen.

"My dad will probably just have him plead guilty or something."

We were at Cedar Lake. It was a few days after the Nissan thing, one of those hot, muggy, windless, semi-cloudy days, and the lake was pretty disgusting in that scummy mid-summer way. It had to get way hotter than it was to make it worth getting in the water with all the algae and stuff, so we were just hanging out on the beach and waiting for Will to show up.

Jen said, "I don't see why a guy like that even deserves a lawyer."

"Well, if we'd got caught stealing that car, I bet my dad would have defended us. Even if we were totally guilty."

"I still can't believe we did that."

"I wish you'd quit saying that," I said, but really I didn't mind — I thought it was cool. I rolled over onto my stomach and rested my chin on my fist and stared at the weave of my towel, imagining myself getting arrested and thrown in a jail cell with a bunch of skanky prostitutes and drug addicts and baby-killers, even though all we did was drive around a little and eat at a Taco Bell. I thought about my parents looking at me through the bars of my cell. My dad saying, *Why on earth would you do such a stupid thing?*

I would tell him it had nothing to do with lack of intelligence.

You've got your whole life ahead of you!

Yeah, Dad, but it was one of those living-in-the-moment things.

The thing he would never understand was that it only had to make sense for about one decision-making nanosecond. Later it might seem moronic, but at the time it all made perfect sense. Anyway, we got away with it. Because for every time some kid like me pays the price for doing something incredibly stupid, there are a thousand times she gets away with it.

"I told Will," Jen said.

"What did he say?"

"'Cool.' He said, 'Cool.'"

"That's all he ever says."

"He's supposed to be here." She sat up and looked around. "There he is."

Will Ford was shuffling shirtless toward us with his size-thirteen flip-flops leaving troughs in the sand. A half-empty twenty-ounce bottle of Mountain Dew dangled by its neck from his long fingers.

"Hey," he said. That was Will's other favorite word. *Hey. Hey, cool. Cool. Hey.* He could express just about any thought with those two words.

"Hey," said Jen.

"Hey," I said.

Will folded his half-naked body onto the sand between our towels.

"Steal any more cars?" Will said.

Okay, I was exaggerating about him only having two words.

"Not today," I said.

"Cool." He gave me a sideways look, like he was seeing someone he didn't know.

"It was a one-time deal," I said.

Will shrugged. "Cool."

I should explain about Will being both my and Jen's boyfriend. Really, he'd been Jen's boyfriend since second grade, but not like her *boyfriend* boyfriend, even though they had made out a couple of times. And then last year I sort of hooked up with him in a closet at this party I wasn't supposed to be at, and Jen found out, and we had this teary three-hour fight. In the end we decided to share him. Neither of us had made out with him since. I should explain about that too. Will was like one of those sex dolls. Not that I've ever *seen* a sex doll, but he was like, *hey, cool, whatever.* I almost had to grab his hands and put them on me. I don't know why I even did that except maybe I was jealous of Jen for having him. But it wasn't any fun because it was like he was kissing me and stuff just to be polite or something and not like he was into it. So we worked it out, me and Jen, and we came to the conclusion that Will just wasn't interested in sex, and that was how it got to be okay that he was both of our boyfriends.

"This guy dropped his keys," I told Will. "I just happened to pick them up, and then later we took his car for a ride. I brought it back, so it wasn't really stealing."

Will nodded. "Know what I'd like to steal? Alton Wright's Hummer."

Jen laughed, and Will's lips turned up in this half smirk that he doesn't do very often.

"That would be fun," I said.

Alton Wright's Hummer was yellow. There is something about yellow cars that is just naturally irritating. And it was a Hummer. Also irritating. And it was Alton's. Alton Wright was one of those people you wanted to do damage to, but you couldn't because he had too many friends. The reason he had friends was because he had a yellow Hummer, and he was smart and funny in a cruel sort of way, and he looked like he should be in a movie. But anyone with any taste whatsoever hated him because he was so full of himself. Especially while driving his yellow Hummer.

So I knew where Will was coming from, but still it surprised me, with Will being so laid-back and all, that he would even think about it.

"He comes into Ducky's," Will said. "I have to vacuum it out like every week." Ducky's Auto Laundry was the car wash and detailing shop where Will worked weekends. "One of these days I'm gonna get a dead rat and hide it in his glove compartment and hope he doesn't find it till it explodes."

That was the longest sentence I'd ever heard from Will.

"Where are you going to get a rat?" I asked.

Will shrugged.

Jen said, "So did you hear that Kell's dad is defending a serial rapist?"

That night I watched *Gone in 60 Seconds* with Nicolas Cage and Angelina Jolie. The idea is that Nicolas Cage is this retired car thief who, for reasons too ridiculous to say, is forced by a bad guy to steal fifty cars in one night, which he does, but of course he has to kill the bad guy in the end, and he saves a cop's life at the same time, so the cop lets him go. I don't know what Angelina Jolie is doing in the movie, but her hair is really weird, and now that you know what happens, you don't have to waste your money renting it unless you *really* like Nicolas Cage, in which case consider yourself warned.

Kelleigh Monahan: five foot seven, a hundred ten curvaceous pounds, thick silky black hair, full lips, perky nose, and sparkling hazel eyes. It's true. Or it would be true if I was wearing stack-heeled boots and hazel contact lenses and a push-up bra, and got collagen injections in my lips. And lost seven pounds.

The perky nose I really have — I got that from my mom — and I do have black hair, which I got from my dad, but it's not all that silky.

Actually, I do not hate the way I look. Sometimes I see actresses on TV who remind me of myself, give or take a few major details like complexion and bust size and so forth. But there is always room for improvement, so for purposes of reading my story you should go with the tall, sleek, puffy-lipped, perky-nosed, hazel-eyed, silky-raven-haired beauty. It's close enough.

When I was nine years old I used to watch this old show called *Flipper* on TV Land. It was about this really smart dolphin who saved the day in every episode. I got all excited about dolphins — or porpoises, as they are also called. So for my tenth birthday my dad gave me a dolphin necklace. It was just a chain with this dolphin carved out of soapstone, but it was nice of him to remember that I liked *Flipper*.

I wore it to school, and of course everybody noticed and said how cool it was. A few days later, this girl Madison who wanted to be my friend gave me a pencil with an eraser shaped like a dolphin. I didn't really want to be her friend because I already had Jen, but I said thank you and used the pencil at school. And then my mom bought me a new bedspread that had jumping dolphins on it. Pretty soon, for birthdays, Christmas, or no reason at all, people were giving me dolphin things and I didn't know how to make them stop. I didn't even like *Flipper* anymore. So one day — it was about a week before my thirteenth birthday — I had a complete dolphin meltdown. I took every dolphin thing I owned and made a pile in the backyard fire pit and poured half a can of gasoline on it. My mom noticed me out there and came out to see what I was doing with my bedspread and stuffed dolphins and dolphin posters and dolphin T-shirts and everything else piled up in the fire pit, and I lit it.

Gasoline is more flammable than I'd thought. There was a huge *whoosh!* and I jumped back, but not quick enough. I ended up losing all the hairs on my right arm, my right eyebrow, and some off my bangs too. Fortunately, my clothes didn't catch on fire. My mom freaked, of course, and so did my dad when he got home. You'd have thought it was the worst thing anybody had ever done in the history of people doing bad things. But I didn't feel all that bad about it until my dad said, "Did you burn the necklace too?"

Actually, it was the one thing I kept. But I didn't tell him that.

I was grounded for a week and they made me see a therapist. After a couple hours of taking tests and talking and crying, the therapist told my parents I was a normal kid who sometimes had difficulty expressing her feelings. She also told them not to give me any more dolphin stuff.

I mention this because it sort of relates to what later happened with Alton Wright's Hummer. Because people just love to know things about you, as in *Kelleigh Monahan has a dolphin fetish* or *Stuey Kvasnick has only one testicle* or *Kathy*

Forest will do it with any guy who smiles at her. Anything that makes you predictable and classifiable, like it gives them a mental file drawer to put you in and forever after that's where they keep you. It only takes one thing for them to create that file.

Even your closest friends.

Will called me up a week after the first car thing and said, "Hey."

"Hey," I said back.

"Doing anything Saturday?"

"Why?"

"I need a favor."

The Hummer dealership was only four blocks from the car wash. The guy at the service counter took the key without looking at me. He asked me my name. I told him it was Cordelia Fink. He set the key on the counter, typed something into his computer, and frowned.

"Did you purchase the vehicle here?"

"It's my boyfriend's. Alton Wright?"

The service guy stared at me for a couple seconds. What he saw was a girl wearing a Minnesota Twins baseball cap (my dad's) that covered up all her arguably silky black hair.

She was also wearing an oversize pair of Gucci sunglasses (my mom's), a baby blue tunic top (also my mom's), and lipstick (which I never wear). I was *incognito*.

The guy typed in Alton's name. He scrolled around a bit, then said, "I've got a *Dennis* Wright."

"That's Alton's dad. The car's probably in his name."

"You know you could have just called this in," he said. "We could have made a new key from the VIN number. Had it ready for you."

"Next time I throw my boyfriend's spare keys in the lake, I'll be sure to do that."

The service guy laughed. "Alton Wright. I remember that kid now," he said. "I don't blame you." He picked up the key. "I'll have Johnny cut you a new one. Take about twenty minutes. He's a little backed up this morning. Make yourself comfortable." He pointed me toward the customer lounge.

I texted Will.

getting key. 20 min.

A few seconds later Will texted me back.

hurry!

When I got to Ducky's, Alton Wright was in the lobby, yelling at the manager. I stopped outside the open door to listen.

"Sir, I'm sure your vehicle will be ready any moment now —"

"Since when does it take an hour for a Speedy Detail?" He pointed at the sign behind the counter. "'In and out in thirty minutes!' That's what the sign says. 'Speedy Detail — Fastest Auto Detail in the Metro.' That's false advertising!"

"If you'll just wait here, sir, I'll go back and find out what's taking them so long —"

"Damn right you will." He looked at his watch. "See if I ever come back here!"

The manager disappeared, and so did I. I didn't think Alton Wright would recognize me — he probably didn't even know who I was in the first place — but why take chances? I ran around the building to the back entrance of the detailing shop. Will was waiting hard.

"What *took* you?" he said, not very nicely. He grabbed Alton's keys from me and ran back into the shop, yelling, "I found them!"

"You're welcome," I said to the air.

Later that same day I called Jen to vent.

"Your boyfriend was rude to me," I said.

"*Your* boyfriend's rude all the time. Maybe we should order a new one."

"From Boyfriends 'R' Us?"

"Or eBay. What did he do?"

I told her about the key thing.

"Why did he want a copy of Alton's key?"

"Don't you remember? He wants to put a dead rat in Alton's Hummer."

"Oh." Even over the phone I could tell she was making a face. "That doesn't sound like something Will would really do."

"Remember last May? Will was walking by the curb and there was this puddle and Alton came driving by and, like, soaked him on purpose. Will was pissed for days."

"Sounds like he's *still* pissed. You think he'll really do it?"

"No. But just knowing he can if he wants to is probably enough. Anyway, I still have the copy of the key."

Which is why I wasn't completely surprised when Will texted me a couple of hours later.

I walked over to Charlie Bean's and found Will at the back table, sipping on an iced coffee. I tossed the duplicate Hummer key on the table in front of him.

"Cool," he said.

"You owe me twenty bucks and a Phrap-o-chino." That was Charlie Bean's quadruple-shot blended espresso drink, the best legal alternative to mainlining crystal meth.

"Cool. Only I'll have to owe you. I'm tapped."

Tapped is normal for Will Ford. He spends all his money on music and games. I bought myself a Phrap-o-chino.

When I got back to the table Will was still staring down at the key.

"Did you find a dead rat yet?" I asked.

"Why would I want a dead rat?"

"I thought you were going to put a dead rat in his car."

"Where would I get a dead rat?"

I shrugged. I was not about to advise him on dead rat procurement.

Will took the straw out of his iced coffee and twisted it into some weird shape — a rattrap, maybe. It took him about a minute of intense twisting and folding, and when he was done, he straightened it, blew through it to puff it out, and put it back in his drink.

"No rat. I need you to help me steal his Hummer."

See what I mean? You steal one car and all of a sudden all your friends decide that's what you are.

"Look," I said, "just because I stole one car — and I didn't really *steal* it; it's more like I *borrowed* it — that doesn't mean I'm your designated car thief. I got the key for you. Steal it yourself."

"I don't know how to drive," he said.

"I don't see how that's my fault. You're the one who didn't take the test."

"My parents think you have to be twenty-five to drive," said Will, all pitiful and hangdog, a look he does particularly well.

"I don't get why you're so pissed at Alton," I said. "I mean,

I know he's a stuck-up jerk, and it was shitty of him to tsunami you, but isn't stealing his Hummer kind of extreme?"

"Why did you think I wanted the key?"

"For the dead *rat*!"

"He's been telling everybody I'm gay."

"Really?" I wanted to ask, *Are you?* But I didn't.

"He told all the guys at Ducky's I'm gay."

"Oh."

"I'm not."

"I wouldn't care if you were," I said.

"The guys, they don't really think I'm gay, but they're having fun giving me shit about it. It's a pain, y'know?"

I could see where that would be a pain.

"That's not all," he said. "You remember when Alton asked Jen out last May?"

"Sure. She said no."

"Well, he's also telling everybody that you and Jen are lesbos. And that I'm like your *beard*."

"I think a beard is a *girl* who dates a gay *guy*."

"Whatever. I just thought it would be fun to borrow his Hummer."

I sucked down the last of my drink. I had to admit, the idea of boosting Alton's Hummer was sounding a little less crazy.

Just for the record, Jen and I are not lesbians.

Roast chicken, wild rice, steamed kale, and a salad. I got away with not eating any kale. The rest of it was pretty good though. My mom can cook.

"You don't have much to say tonight," she said to me.

"I'm thinking about the white whale," I said. "I know it's a metaphor but I don't know what for."

"How far are you in the book?" my dad asked.

"Chapter four. The entire chapter is about a *bedspread*."

He laughed.

"I'm not kidding. And I have a hundred and thirty-one chapters to go."

He laughed harder.

"Did *you* read it?" I asked.

He helped himself to more chicken. "I read the CliffsNotes version."

"Michael!" said my mother.

"*And* I saw the movie," he said with a grin.

"I'm sure you'll get through it," my mother said to me, giving my dad her we-must-set-an-example look.

"Metaphors in famous old books are always about politics," my dad said. "Or sex. I'm sure it will all make sense by the time they get to the harpooning."

"Did you know that everybody thinks we're lesbians?"

"Who?" Jen asked. "Everybody who?" We were talking

on the phone so I couldn't see her, but I could tell from the nasal sound in her voice that she was lying on her back with her head hanging over the edge of the mattress.

"Everybody. Alton Wright's revenge for you not going out with him."

"I couldn't go out with him because my parents have this ridiculous 'no car dates' rule!"

"You're supposed to say it was because you are devoted to Will, our one true love."

"Oh yeah. That too."

"Will wants me to steal Alton's car."

"Really? And do what with it?"

"He has an idea."

I put on my black-on-black auto theft outfit and sneaked out about an hour after midnight. Will was waiting behind the garage.

"Hey," he said, looking me over. "Cool."

"Let's go." We started walking. "Where does he live?" I asked.

"Over by General Mills."

I stopped. "That's like four miles from here!"

"So?"

"You could have told me."

"Sorry."

By the time we got to Alton Wright's house it was two in the morning. The Hummer was parked at the curb, under a streetlamp. All the lights in the house were off. We stood in the shadow of a crabapple tree and looked around to make sure there were no late-night dog walkers or other signs of life. All we saw was a raccoon running across the street. My heart was starting up its mosh pit again. I grabbed Will's hand. It was cold and sweaty.

"If we get caught, this was your idea," I said.

"Okay."

"I can't believe you talked me into this."

"Me neither."

There is no real difference between scared and excited. Think roller coaster. Think first kiss. Think stealing a car.

I don't know what triggered it, but after we stood there saying nothing for about two minutes, I felt my body start to move. A couple of seconds later I was unlocking the car door. I jumped in and stared at a completely unfamiliar set of controls. It took me almost a minute to figure out where the key went. Finally I shoved it in and turned it and felt the engine rumble. Will was banging on the passenger window. I fumbled with the buttons until his door clicked open. He jumped in and we took off.

"Shit, shit, shit," he said. I looked over and he was grinning all across his face.

I knew exactly what he was feeling.

The Pit was a sinkhole in a vacant tract of land just on the other side of the freeway. A few months later it would get turned into a landscaped pond in the middle of a new commercial development, but back then it was a deep hole about a hundred feet across and filled with water. Local legend had it that the hole was five hundred feet deep and there were old cars and dinosaur bones and whatever down at the bottom. It used to be a popular swimming hole, but after years of crazy parties, the number of broken beer bottles reached critical mass and then somebody threw a dead raccoon in there and it floated there for days. Even after it sank, this dead-animal smell sort of hovered over the pond, and after that nobody swam there.

There were a bunch of trees and bushes around most of the pond, but there was one place you could drive right up to the edge. I pulled the Hummer up as close as I dared and stopped. The headlights skimmed the top of the pond; I could see various unidentified things floating there. They looked to me like dead bodies even though I knew they were just plastic bottles and bags and branches and stuff. I turned the lights off and we got out. The muddy, slippery bank below us sloped steeply down to the water ten feet below. A rotten, fishy odor hung in the still air.

"Now what?" I asked.

"Now we test the underwater performance of the Hummer H2," Will said. His voice came out high-pitched.

"I am *not* driving into the water," I said.

"Put it in neutral. We'll push it in."

I don't know how much a Hummer weighs, but there was no way. It was like trying to move a tank.

"Pull it forward," Will said. "Just a little. So the front wheels are over the edge."

It took him a few minutes to talk me into getting back in the car and trying it. I kept one foot on the brake and sort of jerked the Hummer forward a few inches at a time.

"A little farther," Will said. He was standing outside, looking at the front wheels.

The nose of the Hummer was pointing slightly down. I eased up on the brake for just a second and felt the SUV move another couple inches.

"Just a little more," Will said.

Again, I eased up on the brake and felt the front tires go all the way over the edge. I jammed my foot down hard on the brake, but this time the vehicle kept on going, sliding over the lip of the bank, moving slowly but unstoppably down toward the water. I froze with my foot on the brake and my hands locked on the steering wheel. I think I was screaming.

"Stop!" Will shouted. Like I wasn't trying.

The Hummer slewed sideways on the muddy bank and began to tilt to the right. I *know* I was screaming at that point. There was an awful splashy crunch as it tipped onto its side. I fell across the seats and whacked my head against the passenger window as the Hummer slid nose first, on its side, into the water. I flailed around in the dark, trying to figure out which way was up. For some reason my brain wouldn't accept that the driver's side of the SUV was now above me. I could hear Will shouting, but it sounded like he was a mile away, and then water started pouring in through the open window, which actually helped me get my bearings. I twisted around and got my feet on the passenger door and stood up and grabbed the edges of the driver's-side window and pulled myself up. I was half out when Will grabbed me and pulled me all the way and we both fell with a shout into the water, and again I was disoriented, not knowing which way was which, but somehow I got my head back above the water and managed to splash my way to shore, and so did Will, and then we were on the slippery muddy bank spitting and gasping and making retching noises, or at least I was, and Will was going, "Shit, shit, shit!" and then I was sobbing and pummeling him on the shoulder with my fists and all we could see of the Hummer was the left rear taillight sticking up above the scummy brown surface.

That was the closest I ever came to getting killed.

Will walked me all the way home. It was a long, drippy,

squishy walk. For the first part of it we didn't say much, just listened to the *squoosh, squoosh, squoosh* of our wet shoes. Then Will said, "Your squooshing is louder than mine."

"That's because I got wetter," I said.

"I think we both got as wet as is humanly possible."

"Yeah, but I was wetter for longer." I noticed that Will was walking funny, like he was bowlegged. "How come you're walking weird?"

"I'm having crotch problems."

"Explain."

He stopped and tugged at the wet legs of his jeans. "It's like they're climbing up my legs."

I started laughing, then Will was laughing too, and then he was walking with his legs really far apart, swinging them all stiff and holding his arms out in front like a zombie, and we both started laughing even harder.

That lasted about a block.

What was strange was that the whole way home we never talked about what we had done. I kept seeing the image of that one taillight sticking up out of the water, and imagining myself stuck inside the Hummer, all drowned and bloated like the dead raccoon.

It was four-thirty when I sneaked back in. I threw my stinky, sodden clothes in the washer, took a long shower, and went to bed.

"Are you on drugs?" my mother asked me the next morning.

I pulled my bedspread off my face and glared at her.

"I'm just tired."

"It's eleven o'clock. I've already been to my Rotary club meeting, gone grocery shopping, and gotten a haircut."

"Your hair looks nice," I said.

"Thank you." She gave me the Look. "I heard you taking a shower in the middle of the night."

"I couldn't sleep."

She gave me some more of the Look, then said, "Well, it's time to get up." She walked off to perform her next highly productive task, leaving my door standing wide open which she knew I hated. I checked my clock just to make sure she wasn't lying. She *was* lying: It was only 10:53. Which meant I'd had about five hours of sleep. I sniffed. I sniffed again. Something smelled fishy. I sat up and sniffed my arm.

It was *me*. Rotten fish–smell girl. I'd thought I'd washed it all off when I got home, but the nose-wrenching aroma of *eau de pit* had penetrated my pores. I got out of bed, headed for the shower, and promised myself that I would never, ever let Will or anybody else talk me into doing anything stupid ever again as long as I lived.

Ha.

I spent the next few days half expecting a SWAT team to surround the house and arrest me for Hummer-drowning, but nothing happened — except that four days later Alton Wright was driving a brand-new Toyota FJ, eyeball-searing orange, paid for by his parents. So it was almost like we had done him a favor. Will went back to his original plan, saying he was going to find a dead rat someplace and hide it in Alton's spare-tire compartment.

"Why not a dead squirrel?" Jen said. "They're easier to find."

"It has to be a rat," said Will.

———

There are many reasons to steal a car. The most common reason is because the car thief needs to get someplace, and a car is the best way to do that. Other reasons to steal a car are money, thrills, and revenge. If you steal a car to get back at somebody, though, you are probably only getting back at their insurance company.

———

I heard my mother say once that the hardest part of being a parent is not knowing which of the things you say to your kids is going to stick. Well, relax, Mom. Ninety-nine percent of it doesn't. But still, I knew what she meant, because that little remark my dad made about reading the CliffsNotes version of *Moby-Dick* — I don't even know if he was kidding or not — really got to me. I mean, there I was struggling with "Call me Ishmael" (the lamest opening line since "In the beginning . . ."), with five-hundred-some pages to go, and my dad tells me I'm more or less wasting my time. Unless he was kidding, which he might have been. So I was a little peeved at him and ready to give him a taste of the silent treatment when he got home, but he was all stoked over the latest development in the Elwin Carl Dandridge case and didn't notice me being pointedly sullen.

"I'm going to get it thrown out of court," he said to my mother, pouring himself a celebratory scotch on the rocks.

"That's wonderful!" she said. I was surprised she didn't jump up and down and clap her hands.

I, crushed into the sofa by the weight of *Moby-Dick*, turned the page. I was on chapter fifteen — a hundred twenty to go — and Ishmael still hadn't met Captain Ahab, let alone any white whales, but he had a lot to say about clam chowder — an entire chapter, actually. My father's verbal victory dance, disgusting as it was, was far more interesting.

One of the private investigators who worked for my dad's law firm had turned up a witness who claimed that he and Elwin Carl Dandridge were partying at some bar downtown at the exact same time victim number seven was being raped in the back stairwell of her dormitory. The witnesses even had a cell phone shot of Dandridge standing at the bar in front of a TV that was showing a baseball game. According to my dad, the particular game on the TV — once they got their experts to testify which inning of which game it was — would corroborate the witness's testimony, proving that Dandridge was not the rapist.

"I thought they had his DNA," I said.

"They do! That's what makes it so great. If he couldn't have done that one rape because he was someplace else, then *all* their DNA evidence for *all* the rapes becomes suspect. And best of all, the bar he was in is a *gay* bar."

"What difference does that make?"

"Well, if Dandridge is gay, then why would he go around raping girls?"

"But . . . he's *guilty*, right?"

"If he was someplace other than the scene of the crime, then no."

"But what about all the *other* rapes?"

He shrugged and sipped his drink.

"That sucks!" I said.

"Kelleigh!" said my mother.

"Well, it does. What if he gets off and then rapes *me*?"

"I'm sure that won't happen," my mother said.

My dad swirled his scotch, listening to the ice cubes clinking the sides of the glass.

That night I couldn't sleep. I kept smelling dead fish, so around one o'clock I changed my sheets and took another shower and got dressed and decided to go for a walk in the middle of the night. On the way out the back door I noticed my dad's car keys hanging there, so instead of going for a walk I took my dad's Lexus for a drive.

I didn't really think about it much; I just grabbed the keys and went. Almost like it was a normal thing to do. I didn't even think about what my dad would do if he caught me.

There are thirty or forty lakes in the Twin Cities area. I drove around seven of them and only got lost once. It was a quiet, dark night with hardly any traffic and no moon. Very peaceful. I didn't even turn on the radio. I just drove until the gas gauge was on empty, then went home. It wasn't nearly as exciting as stealing somebody's car for real, but it felt good to be driving around on my own. When I got home I poured most of the gas from my dad's lawn mower gas can into the car so he wouldn't notice that his car was suddenly on empty. Then I sat on the front porch for a while. It smelled like roses and cigarette butts. The rose-bushes were sort of a hobby of my mom's. The cigarette butts that littered the ground between the roses and the house were my mom's too. She had been sneaking smokes ever since I could remember. My dad and I never said anything about it.

I sat there for like an hour, then went inside and took another shower and climbed into bed and fell asleep almost right away.

Just so you don't get the idea that I have only two friends and that we are locked in some weird sexless triangle, I should tell you about the Vails.

Jon and Jim Vail are almost twins, but not quite. They were born ten and a half months apart, but they are both starting twelfth grade in the fall. Jon, the older one, is Will's big sister's ex-boyfriend, and Jim is the one Jen had a secret crush on and the one I once almost had sex with in the basement of his house — and I maybe would have, except his mom started yelling something down the stairs and we freaked and quit doing what we'd been about to do.

I guess Jen and I have exactly the same taste in guys.

That thing in the Vails' basement happened way back in May, and Jim and I hadn't really talked since. I'd seen him a few times, but he was like, "Hey, how's it going?" without any hint that he actually cared. I guess I acted pretty much the same, so I was surprised when he called and asked if I wanted to drive up to Taylors Falls with him and Candy Cohen and Jason Harris — Jason had a car — to go cliff-jumping, or what passes for cliff-jumping in Minnesota. I'd never been to Taylors Falls, so I said sure.

I didn't mention it to Jen.

Jen Hoffman has been my best friend for almost my entire life. When I was nine and got pneumonia and had to spend six days in the hospital and two weeks at home after that, she came to visit me every single day. She loaned me her entire collection of Anne of Green Gables books, and her iPod, and she even brought me Mr. Poo, my stuffed poodle, who I'd had since I was four. I was way too old for Mr. Poo even then, but it was super-nice of Jen to ask my mom to dig him out of the closet where he'd been hiding in a box with a bunch of other stuffed toys I'd grown out of but still sort of missed. That's how Jen is. Even when we fight I always know she'll be my best friend forever. We made a sacred pact to be each other's bridesmaids, no matter what. In fact, we even talked about moving to Utah and marrying a polygamist so we could have the same husband. Like with Will — only for real.

Jim Vail was a different deal. He was Jen's secret, and even I wasn't supposed to know about her thing for him. And it turned out he was my secret too, after that one time in his parents' basement, which was when I found out about him and Jen.

The way it happened was I was walking through Bassett's Creek Park on my way to the SuperAmerica and Jim was there playing frisbee golf with one of his friends. I sort of slowed down to watch and Jim threw a frisbee at me. He said later he meant to throw it *to* me, but I wasn't ready for it and it hit me right in the forehead. Big drama with tears and a welt on my forehead and accusations and so forth.

I'd known Jim for years. We live just a couple of blocks apart. But until recently our two-year age difference had put us in different worlds. So it was interesting having him hovering over me and touching my shoulder and apologizing and for once treating me as if I actually existed. We started talking. His friend got bored and took off but Jim and I stayed and talked for a long time and then he suggested we walk over to his place so I could see their seven new puppies.

You're probably thinking, *Uh-oh. Older Boy uses puppies to lure Sweet Young Thing into his lair of Depravity and Sexual Excess.* But it wasn't like that at all. Jim was extremely polite and chivalrous and never touched me except to put some ointment on my frisbee wound. The puppies, golden retrievers, were amazing, three weeks old and all tongues, ears, milk teeth, soft paws, and sweet puppy breath. They crawled over and around me for a frantic half hour while Jim just sat in his dad's TV chair and laughed and watched.

"You want one?" he asked.

Oh. My. God. Did I ever want one! But of course I couldn't, what with my dad being allergic and all.

I said I would think about it. And I did. I thought of nothing else. I knew there was no way, but I just had to see them again so I went over to the Vails' again the next day for another dose of puppy breath.

That was when Jim told me about Jen.

It's always kind of strange to learn that your closest friend, who you share *everything* with — like Super-embarrassing Moments, and Dreams for the Future, and Worst Fears — has a secret. I mean, I have secrets from Jen, I guess, but nothing like the secret I found out about that day from Jim Vail, which was that Jen had been calling his cell number like five times a day and then hanging up when he answered.

Caller ID is a bad thing for stalkers. Back before I was born, you could call somebody up and when they answered you could hang up and they would never know it was you. But now all they have to do is check their caller ID. Yeah, I know you can block your number from showing up by dialing whatever-whatever, but here's the thing: Stalkers do not think rationally. I guess secretly they want the harassed person to know who is doing the harassing. At least that was true in Jen's case, and I could even kind of understand it a little because Jim Vail is majorly good-looking and two years older than us and therefore both unavailable and highly desirable.

It's one thing to flirt with a couple of college boys at the country club pool, but another thing altogether to hook up with an older boy who happens to live in your neighborhood and whose parents know your parents, so the way I figure it, Jen was obsessed enough to dial Jim's number repeatedly, but not crazy enough to actually talk to him. Unlike me.

What Jim Vail said to me as I wrestled with the puppies was "Hey, why don't you tell your little friend to quit calling me?"

"What little friend?"

"Jen Hoffman."

Then he told me about getting all those calls, and I just kept saying, "Wow," while thinking about the utter weirdness of the whole situation.

And then, just to confuse me even more, he told me he liked my hair and said I should never cut it even if it grew all the way down my back to my legs. And then — I'm not sure how it happened — he was kissing me, and even though I'd never thought about him that much before, I was totally into it. I mean, in my heart and soul I gave up my virginity right then even though technically I still was one, thanks to Mrs. Vail yelling down the stairs about sixty seconds before I might not have been.

All that happened before Jen and I stole the Nissan. I never said a word to Jen, and she never told me about her stalking Jim Vail via cell phone, and so as far as anybody knew we were both still faithful to each other and to our possibly-gay boyfriend Will.

But now Jim wanted me to go up to Taylors Falls with him.

———————

Tuesday morning I was awake but still in bed when my mom peeked into my room, then came in and sat down on the end of my bed with this scary blank expression on her face. She put her hand on the bedspread and sort of squeezed my leg, and my heart started beating in my ears like *whoosh-chunka-whoosh* because I knew she was about to tell me something really awful. Like they were getting a divorce. Or somebody got cancer.

"What?" I said.

"Honey . . ."

That was bad. The last time she'd called me "Honey" was when she'd told me Chipper had died. Chipper was our beagle. Later I learned that he hadn't really died. They had given him away to my dad's second cousin in Alexandria, because my dad couldn't handle all the sneezing and red eyes. He said it made him look like a sick drug addict in court. But still, they didn't have to lie to me.

"Your grandmother passed away last night."

"Which one?"

"Grandma Kate."

I breathed out a sigh of relief. I'd been afraid she was talking about my other grandmother, Grandma Gail, who I liked.

I'd known for a long time that Grandma Kate, my dad's mom, was sick with emphysema and needed an oxygen tank. She and Grandpa John lived way up in Danbury, Wisconsin.

I didn't like her much anyway. That sounds really cold, I know, but all she ever did was wheeze and cough and criticize me and my mom and anybody else who came in range. I hadn't seen her for a while, because lately she'd been too sick to travel. Then I had this weird thought that maybe they'd put Grandma Kate in some sort of home and were just telling me she was dead.

"The funeral is on Friday," my mom said.

Friday was the day I was supposed to go to Taylors Falls with Jim. My face must have done something, because my mom leaned toward me and said, "Oh, honey, she was ready to go."

I nodded, still thinking about Taylors Falls. I was disappointed, but at the same time I was a little bit relieved.

"How's Grandpa John?" I asked. I liked Grandpa John.

"Pretty good, considering. He and your dad talked for a long time this morning. I think in a way he's at peace — he and Kate had a tough last couple of years. I guess for the last few months she couldn't even get out of bed to go to the bathroom." My mom looked into my eyes. "Don't ever smoke," she said, squeezing my leg hard.

I don't smoke. I don't drink except for just a couple times. I don't do drugs. I don't shoplift or vandalize public property or cheat on tests or sell my body or eat with my elbows on the table or pee in the swimming pool.

Grandma Kate's funeral was on the hottest day of the summer, ninety-one degrees in Danbury, Wisconsin, which is way up north in the pine trees, where it's supposed to stay cool. Two old people had to be escorted out of the church all woozy from heatstroke or something. Everybody was using their funeral programs to fan themselves. The coffin had an enormous spray of roses on top with all the blossoms pointing in different directions. One of them was pointed directly at me. I imagined that every rose was pointed exactly at somebody and that if you knew the language of roses, they would tell you what day you were going to die.

Later at the grave site, instead of huddling right up next to the grave like they did at my great-aunt's funeral, people spread out to stand under trees where there was some shade. But my mom and dad and I had to endure the preacher's ashes-to-ashes routine under the full sun. By the time it was over I was feeling kind of woozy myself. When we got back to Grandpa John's, I drank three glasses of cold cider one right after another.

About thirty people showed up for the after-funeral party, which was mostly on the screen porch and outside on the lawn where they'd set up a canopy in case it rained. Except for two babies and a couple of six-year-olds, I was the youngest person there by about twenty years, so after scarfing down some funeral food (Swedish meatballs, sliced ham, potato salad, chips, brownies), I went inside and wandered through the house. Grandma Kate's room was on the first floor right next to the bathroom. Grandpa John had set it up like a hospital, with the big metal bed and a walker and a bedside tray covered with bottles of pills and Kleenex and a few quilting magazines, even though I don't think she'd been doing much quilting lately. I sat down in the chair by the bed, where my grandfather probably used to sit a lot listening to her wheezy complaints. It was sad.

After that I went to my grandfather's room upstairs and sat on his neatly made bed and tried to imagine what it was like to be an old man with a dead wife. The books by his bed were all about sailing and flying. As far as I knew, he had never done either. That was sad too. I picked up the phone on his nightstand and called Jen — I'd forgotten my cell phone at home — but I only got her voicemail.

Because we were immediate family, we had to stay until everybody else left. I was afraid we might have to stay overnight and I got this idea that they might make me sleep in Grandma Kate's bed, which would be way too weird, so I went outside and looked at all the cars parked in front and fantasized about driving off in one. I could drive down to Taylors Falls and meet up with Jim and Jason and Candy — except that Jim had probably invited some other girl after I told him I couldn't come.

There was this sporty little Miata convertible that belonged to Angie Wingert, my dad's brother's sister-in-law. The top was down. I opened the door. The car started beeping the way cars do when you leave the keys in. Sure enough, there they were, dangling from the ignition. I guess Angie figured that way out in the country with only family and friends around, what was there to worry about?

I put my hands on the wheel and imagined driving off with the hot wind whipping my hair, looking good. I turned on the stereo. She'd been listening to a Celine Dion CD. I turned it off fast, got out of the car, and went back inside. I had no intention of stealing my aunt-in-law's car in broad daylight at my grandmother's funeral, but it was fun to think about.

The reason I'm telling all this stuff about my grandmother's funeral is because of how it made me feel like I was living in a completely different reality from everybody else, like I was a ghost or a half-real creature from a parallel universe. A few times, one or another of the adults would notice me and say something like "You must be Michael's daughter. What grade are you in?" As if they were checking to see how long it would be before I became fully human. The only person I could relate to at all was Grandpa John, and I only got to talk to him for like thirty seconds before we were interrupted, but he did say one cool thing to me. He said, "I bet you can't wait to get the hell out of here."

I looked at him all shocked, because we were supposed to be having all this somber, mopey togetherness. He burst out laughing.

"Listen," he said, "when I was your age, the last thing on earth I wanted to do on a nice summer day was hang out with a bunch of fossils eating Swedish meatballs. So thanks for coming, kid. I appreciate it, I really do. It's great to see you." He stared at my face until I started to get uncomfortable, then gave my shoulder a squeeze and looked away. He said, "You know, Kelleigh, I wish you'd known your grandmother when she was young. Before she got sick."

Then somebody came up to him and said something and he disappeared back into the other world, and a couple hours later we said goodbye and drove back to the Cities.

Three days later a package with my name on it arrived from Grandpa John. Inside was an old color photo: a girl with long, dark hair wearing cutoff denim shorts and a halter top, standing in front of a Volkswagen Beetle. There was a cigarette in her hand. I could see the ocean in the background.

Scrawled in the margin were the words: *Kate - Venice Beach - 1967.*

Except for the cigarette and the denim, she looked exactly like me.

I knew that my grandfather had hitchhiked to California the summer after he graduated from high school. He met my future grandmother Kate at a rock concert in Monterey, and they traveled up and down the West Coast, and for a whole summer nobody heard from them until they showed up unannounced on Christmas Eve. It was one of those old family stories that I'd heard when I was a little kid, but nobody talked about it anymore. Once you're a teenager, adults stop talking about the crazy stuff they used to do, and they start acting as if they were raised by the Amish. But one time I snooped in my grandmother's scrapbook and guess what? According to the dates on their wedding photos, she had married my grandpa John in January 1968. My dad had been born four months later.

I wondered if she had been pregnant that day at Venice Beach.

I stole the Cadillac out of necessity. It was Jen's fault.

When we got home from Grandpa John's after the funeral — it was about eleven — I found six texts on my cell, all from Jen, and every one of them started out with

HELP

I called her right away.

"Are you kidding me?" I said when she answered.

"No! Kell, you gotta come get me. I'm like *marooned* here in freaking Taylors Falls and I don't know anybody and I'm sitting in this weird drive-in and they keep *looking* at me. I think they're going to kick me out. And I don't have any money or *anything*."

I asked her what happened, and she told me.

Just like I'd thought. After I had told Jim I couldn't go to Taylors Falls, he'd found somebody else, and that somebody else turned out to be Jen. Of course she said yes. So they drove up there, her and Jim and Jason and Candy. Jen said it was fun for a while. Jason had a cooler full of beer and they just hung out and drank it and watched a bunch of guys jump off the rocks into the St. Croix. Jim and Jason kept talking about jumping, but it looked way scary and they never did it. But they did all go swimming, and then, according to Jen, Jim started acting all weird and saying things about her body and stuff, "— except it wasn't nice stuff, it was sort of creepy and mean. Like he kept calling me *little girl* and stuff, and asking me if my breasts were the same size or different, and making jokes that only he and Jason thought were funny."

"That doesn't sound like Jim."

"You've never seen him after about six beers."

"What about Candy?" I asked. Candy is a year older than us but younger than Jim and Jason.

"She was pretending she was bored. And then Jim started getting really loaded and so did Jason, and it was getting dark and they were trying to get Candy and me to go skinny-dipping and Jim kept trying to feel me up, but not in a nice way, more like monkey-groping. And I wouldn't go skinny-dipping and neither would Candy and finally Candy got really mad and told Jason to take us home, except I wouldn't get in the car with them 'cause Jason was totally shit-faced. So they just *left* me here. My mom's gonna kill me. I told her I was going to hang out with you. I can't call her. You have to come and get me."

"How am I supposed to do that?"

"Can't you sneak out with your dad's car? Like you did before?"

I had to say yes. Because it was Jen.

The Lexus keys were not hanging in their usual place by the back door. I knew where they probably were: in my dad's pants pocket. In my parents' bedroom. I had this icky feeling that he'd somehow figured out I'd taken his car for a drive, and that was why he hadn't hung up his keys in the usual place. But then I decided it was probably just a coincidence, because if he knew I'd taken his car he would have yelled at me. So I decided to take my mom's Camry, but she always kept her keys in her purse, and that was also in their bedroom. Even if they were asleep, my dad would wake up the instant I opened his door. He was like that.

I was about to call Jen back and tell her I couldn't come, when I remembered the Hallsteds' green Cadillac.

This doesn't have anything to do with anything, but it would seem weird if I didn't mention that the Hallsteds' green Cadillac might not actually be green. I am a deuteranope. That means I'm red-green color-blind, so when I say the Hallsteds' Cadillac was green, it might actually have been red, or when I say Jen was wearing a pink top, it might actually have been light green. A lot of the time I just guess what color things are and it's surprising how often I am right, even when a color just looks *gred* or *reen* to me. Usually I can tell red from green because I know what color things are supposed to be. Grass and lettuce are green; stop signs and apples are red. Unless the apple is green.

What most people don't get is that deuteranopes see just as many colors as regular people. My dad — who is also color-blind — explained it this way: Deuteranopes see an infinite number of colors. There is an infinite number of blues and yellows, and we see those colors just fine. So even if red looks like *gred* or *reen*, we still see more colors than anyone could ever count. A deuteranope's infinity of colors is just different.

By the way, my deuteranopia is one reason I dress the way I do. It's a lot easier to get dressed if you don't have to ask somebody what color your socks are.

I should also mention that color blindness is rare in girls. You have to get the gene from both parents. My dad told me I should feel special, but mostly I don't think about it, which is why I didn't think to mention it until now.

The Hallsteds are an older couple who live next door to us, but in the summer they spend most of their time at their cabin up on Lake Vermilion. They always leave a key with us just in case there's an emergency, like a broken pipe or a tree falling on the house or something. The Hallsteds have two cars: an SUV that they drive up to their cabin, and a Cadillac — possibly green — that stays in their garage.

The key to their house was hanging on our key rack, right next to where my dad's Lexus key was supposed to be.

It took me a while. First the key didn't work in their front door, so I had to go around to the back. Then I had to find the keys to the Cadillac, and that took me forever because instead of hanging them up someplace like normal people, the Hallsteds put them in a *drawer*. The garage was a problem too. I couldn't figure out how to get the electric door to open. There's usually a button, right? But there was no button, just a bunch of switches that turned lights on and off, and I got worried that somebody would see lights flashing in the supposedly vacant Hallsted place.

I finally figured out to use the remote control in the car. Duh.

So the garage door went up and the lights came on, not just in the garage but the outside lights too — a string of them all along each side of the driveway, like, *Look! Look, everybody! Somebody is stealing the Hallsteds' car!*

I backed out fast and closed the door with the remote and hoped nobody had called the police.

I knew Taylors Falls was about fifty miles north of St. Paul, but I didn't know exactly where, and of course the Hallsteds did not have a map in their car, which was ridiculous.

I drove north on I-35 until I got out of the city, then stopped at a gas station and bought a map for $4.95 that Jen was going to owe me for. I was thinking of all the nasty things I was going to say to her when I realized that I didn't have to wait — I had my cell with me. But when I called Jen's cell it shunted me over to her voicemail. I hung up. And then I started to worry. Because Jen is a person who would never, ever let a ringing phone go unanswered.

Jen had told me she was at the Frostop drive-in.

"There's only like one street here. You can't miss it."

Taylors Falls was only a few blocks long. It took me about thirty seconds to find the Frostop, an old-fashioned drive-in, kind of fun and trashy-looking, with a giant mug of root beer for a sign. No lights, no people, no cars. I pulled in, parked, and got out and looked around.

No Jen.

"Jen!" I shouted. My voice sounded small and loud at the same time. Jen didn't answer.

Where would she go? I mean, assuming she hadn't been kidnapped, or raped and killed, or worse.

I tried calling her again. No answer.

I had no idea what to do, so I got in the car and sat there for a while, but that was both boring and nerve-racking, so I drove around the block with the window rolled down. I noticed some lights about three blocks away. A gas station. I drove over and pulled in and there she was slumped against the wall by a Mountain Dew machine, looking like the sorriest homeless girl you ever saw.

According to Jen (I'm going to shorten this because it took her half an hour to tell it), they kicked her out of the Frostop right after she talked to me, and then she hung around on the street for a while, but these nasty-looking guys in a pickup drove by twice, the second time real slow, and they were staring at her, so she ran down to the gas station. She tried to call me again but her cell was dead.

"I knew you'd find me," she said.

"You're welcome," I said.

Jen looked around the Cadillac as if she was seeing it for the first time.

"Hey," she said, "I thought your dad had a Lexus."

I don't know how long the police car had been following us. I had just turned off the freeway and we were driving east on Thirty-sixth when I finally noticed it. I was pretty sure I hadn't done anything wrong, but he was right behind me. I hoped I didn't have a burned-out taillight or anything.

I said to Jen, "Don't look, but there's a police car behind us."

She turned and looked. "Omigod," she said.

"I said, *don't look*."

She turned back around and slumped low in her seat. "Omigod," she said.

I couldn't keep my eyes off the rearview mirror. Waiting for his lights to start flashing. We were coming up to the intersection by Cub Foods when the traffic light turned yellow. I had enough time to make it through the light. The police car behind me had to stop. I was just starting to breathe normally when I saw his lights begin to flash, and he drove right through the red light and came after us.

I turned left at the first side street and punched it.

Some people think Cadillacs are grandma-grandpa cars, but the Hallsteds' Cadillac took off so fast my head slammed back into the headrest. Jen let out a shriek. I made a screeching right turn at the end of the block just as the police car turned off Thirty-sixth, then another quick right into an alley and I punched it again. I wasn't looking at the speedometer but Jen told me later we were going seventy miles an hour down that alley. When we got to the end I had to slam on the brakes. I thought the car was going to roll over when I skidded out onto Thirty-sixth and almost smashed into a minivan. There was no sign of the cop. I made a quick left onto Regent and just kept going straight, blowing through three stop signs without even slowing down, until I was sure we'd lost him.

Have I mentioned that Jen was screaming in my ear the whole time?

————

In movies, stealing cars looks very dramatic and exciting with lots of high-speed chases and screeching tires, but in real life it is something that happens quickly and quietly and mostly nobody notices except that the car is gone. But sometimes even the most careful car thieves must go to extreme measures to get away from the police. It is this possibility that makes auto theft so exciting.

————

We left the car in the parking lot of a dental clinic — not the one I go to. Jen only had to walk a few blocks to get home. I had to walk almost a mile, and when I got there with my right ear still ringing from her screaming, I saw a cop car at the end of the block, sitting at the curb with the lights off. He must have gotten the license number off the Hallsteds' Cadillac and was watching their house. I stood behind the Frankels' garden shed to see what he was going to do. After about twenty minutes, he turned on his headlights and pulled up in front of the Hallsteds' and got out and rang their bell. Then he went back to his car and sat there for a few more minutes before driving away.

I sneaked back into the Hallsteds' and put the car key back in the drawer. It was four-thirty by the time I crawled into bed. Four hours later my mom woke me up to go to our mother-daughter Pilates class.

Our Pilates instructor was a woman named Pilar who was, I think, half Mexican and half android from the future. No matter what she did — even some impossible-to-look-good-doing-it thing like scratching her butt — she did it gracefully. Also she was seventy years old and looked forty. My mom was thirty-nine years old and looked twenty-nine, so I am expecting to age gracefully as well. Pilates is supposed to help because even if you get all wrinkly or flabby or bald you can still stand up straight and do things like bend over to pick up a penny, even though it isn't worth it for just one penny. Pilar could practically make that penny jump off the floor into her hand. Pilates is all about knowing where your center is.

The class was my mom's idea, of course — once again, she'd read a book or article about successful parenting that said mother-daughter activities produced healthy bonding. I'm not making fun of my mom. She means well, and we both like the Pilates class. It gives us a few minutes to talk on the way there and back, but we don't have to talk at all during the class. Pilar had some good ideas too, like that it helps to visualize an action before trying to do it. You imagine yourself bending like a pretzel and pretty soon you can practically tie yourself in a knot. She liked to say, "Head," pointing at her head, "then core," pointing at her center.

That day my mom let me drive home. I backed out of the parking stall, pulled out onto the street, and brought the car smoothly up to precisely thirty miles per hour.

"You're getting very good," she said.

"I've been practicing."

"You have? With Dad?"

"In my head," I said. "Driving the car in my head. Just like Pilates."

Jen had left me a couple texts I ignored, being somewhat perturbed at her for a number of reasons that I hadn't had time to sort out yet, mostly having to do with her going to Taylors Falls with Jim Vail and then making me risk going to jail to come get her and then screaming in my ear so loud my right ear rang for hours. I was stewing over that instead of reading while slumped in the big chair in the TV room with

Moby-Dick in my lap (Pilar would have shaken her head gracefully and told me to align my neck and shoulders) when my mom summoned me to assist in her latest culinary effort by going to Byerly's for some capers.

"The little tiny ones," she said, handing me a five-dollar bill. "The ones about the size of a peppercorn."

"Can I take the car?"

"Ha-ha. No."

"I'll be super-careful. It's only six blocks."

"All the more reason to walk," she said.

"What if they cost more than five dollars?"

She rolled her eyes, then took her five back and gave me a twenty.

"I'll expect change," she said.

I noticed as I was leaving that there was a white card stuck on the Hallsteds' front door. I walked over and looked at it. It was a small envelope from the police department. I put it in my pocket to give to my dad later.

After buying a jar of capers for $4.65, I walked over to Charlie Bean's and ordered a Phrap-o-chino. I figured it might power me through another twenty pages of *Moby-Dick*. My plans for Ishmael, however, were interrupted by one Deke Moffet, the most disreputable member of the soon-to-be senior class. Except he wasn't really a member anymore. He'd dropped out last spring.

"Hey, did you pay for that drink or steal it?" he asked.

Deke was sitting at a table with Marshall Cassidy, the second-most-disreputable member of the soon-to-be senior class. I had always made it a point to never associate with either of them, but it wasn't like me to ignore someone who had spoken to me.

"I don't know what you're talking about," I said.

Deke and Marshall were your standard-issue middle-class suburban juvenile delinquents — not recently shaven, longish hair, rock 'n' roll T-shirts, jeans with possibly authentic rips and stains, and a few hunks of cheap silver jewelry in their ears and probably elsewhere. Deke was kind of muscley and not bad-looking, and Marshall was thin and hard and nervous like a whippet. They weren't exactly scary unless you were scared of teens in general, but you wouldn't want either of them to watch your purse while you went for a swim.

Deke looked at Marshall and they both started laughing.

That was when I should have walked away. Instead, I asked them what was so funny.

"It's just you don't look like a booster," Deke said. "You look more like a Young Republican."

"Church-choir girl," Marshall added.

"What's a *booster*?" I asked.

"You know — *booster*," Deke said, like if he kept repeating it, it might mean something to me. When I still didn't catch on, he said, "Somebody who steals cars."

"You're crazy," I said, and turned away so they couldn't see my face turn red.

Deke called after me, "If you ever want to pick up a little extra money, you just let me know."

I walked home clutching the jar of capers in one hand and my Phrap-o-chino in the other, trying to figure out what to do. Only two people besides me knew about me stealing cars: Jen and Will. One of them had to have told Deke. And I'd have bet my life it wasn't Will, because Will hated Deke Moffet almost as much as he hated Alton Wright.

Which meant I was going to have to strangle Jen.

It turned out that capers are little green pickled flower buds that are an essential ingredient in something called veal piccata, which is thin slices of teenage cow sautéed and served with a lemon-caper sauce and pasta on the side. My dad went crazy over it. He is always quite good at offering praise. Even when dinner is not so good, he finds something nice to say. As for me, I did not enjoy it much. Too sour. I don't think the capers helped, and neither did the subject of Elwin Carl Dandridge, which my dad was completely obsessed with and couldn't stop talking about even at the dinner table. My mom was wearing her adoring-wife face, smiling between tiny bites of lemony, capery veal.

The judge in the Dandridge case had ruled that the bad DNA result (since they supposedly had found Dandridge's DNA on a victim he supposedly couldn't possibly have raped because he had been watching baseball at a gay bar at the time) was not sufficient cause to rule out the DNA evidence from the *other* rapes. My dad was pretty peeved — he said some nasty things about the judge — but he'd also come up with a new angle on the whole deal. He'd found out that Elwin Carl Dandridge had a twin brother who lived in Shakopee, just twenty miles away. Even better, the brother had a record for sexual harassment.

Maybe you don't know this, but identical twins have identical DNA.

"How come it took you so long to find out he had a twin?" I asked.

"They were both adopted. By different families." He cut a wedge of veal and coaxed a few capers onto it with the tip of his knife. "Even Dandridge didn't know he had a twin until two years ago — they were separated at birth." He put the capery veal into his mouth.

"Does this mean that raping is genetic?" I asked.

"Oh, Kelleigh!" said my mother. "Sexual harassment is not *rape*."

"This is absolutely delicious, Annie," my father said.

"If they're both perverts and they're twins, doesn't that mean something?" I asked.

"Not necessarily. It would certainly not be something I'd bring up in court. John Britton — the twin — drives a delivery van, so he drives all over town. He only has a solid alibi for one of the rapes."

"Do you think he did it?" I asked. "The twin?"

My dad shrugged. "The fact that a twin exists casts doubt on Dandridge's guilt." He cut another piece of veal. I noticed that he always cut triangles, whereas my mother cut her veal into rectangles. I looked at my own plate and wondered how I cut the meat. I could not remember. I picked up my knife and fork and pushed the tines of the fork into the thin slice of teenage cow and sawed at it with the knife, detaching a strip of meat. I guess I'm a strip cutter. I scraped off the lemon sauce and the capers and put it into my mouth and chewed. I wondered if I had a twin. I wondered if she was color-blind. Maybe I was secretly adopted and I had a twin who was out there stealing cars — that is, if criminal behavior, unlike meat cutting, was genetic.

When I called her after dinner, Jen swore she never said a word to anybody about me stealing cars. I couldn't see her face, but usually I could tell if Jen was lying, which she does sometimes. From the sound of her voice, I didn't think she was lying this time.

"By the way," I said, "the police were waiting at the Hallsteds' when I got home last night."

I could hear her suck her breath in.

"They left a note on the door," I said.

"What did you do?"

"I gave the note to my dad."

"What did *he* do?"

"He just read it and didn't say anything. I think he doesn't want to worry me. You know, about there being dangerous criminals in the neighborhood. So you're sure you didn't say anything to anybody?"

"No!"

Which left Will.

I rehearsed calling up Will and accusing him of telling Deke Moffet that I was a car thief. It didn't play. For one thing, Will had *despised* Deke Moffet ever since Deke pantsed him in seventh grade right in the school foyer with like a million people watching. And even if he hadn't hated Deke, I just couldn't see Will blabbing to anybody.

I dialed his cell number.

"Hey," he answered.

"Hey," I said. "What's up?"

"Not much."

"My dad's figured out a new way to get his pet rapist back on the street."

"Cool."

This was why I didn't call Will on the phone very often.

I said, "So . . . have you talked to Deke Moffet lately?"

"Why would I do that?"

"I don't know. *Have* you?"

"No. Why?"

"I just thought you might have mentioned something to somebody about Alton's Hummer."

"Nope."

"You haven't said anything to *anybody*?"

"Nope."

I believed him. Unlike Jen, Will Ford did not lie.

I said, "I think Deke knows we did it." I put the *we* in there mostly because I didn't want to be alone, although for all I knew the car theft that Deke had found out about could have been the Nissan or the Cadillac. Or he might even have seen me that night driving around in my dad's Lexus.

Will said, "That's not good."

The next day I saw Marshall at Charlie Bean's again. He looked all pale and red-eyed and jerky, like he was on his hundredth cup of espresso. He was playing a game on his cell phone, moving these little blocks around. His fingernails were gnawed to the bleeding point. It made me all squeamy inside to look at him.

I asked him why he and Deke thought I was a car thief.

"Deke said you deep-sixed Wright's Hummer," he said, not looking up from his game.

"Well, it's not true."

Marshall shrugged, intent on his game.

"Why would he say that?"

"Ask him. *Shit!*" He slammed his palm down on the table. "Level seven!"

Like I would know what he was talking about.

"Where can I find him?" I asked.

Marshall shrugged again, then said, "I bet you could catch him at the mall. Food court." He grinned, showing me his scummy teeth. "Look around, you'll spot him."

Marshall was right. Deke was sitting at one of the bench tables in the food court with a slice of sausage pizza and a Red Bull. I walked up just as he took an enormous bite.

"Hey, if it isn't the booster girl," he said, not bothering to chew and swallow first. "I hear you been stalking me."

I raised my eyebrows.

"Marsh called and warned me," he said.

I sat down across from him.

"So what's up?" he asked.

"I want to know what makes you think I stole a car."

I waited as he finished his slice and washed it down with Red Bull. He was enjoying himself.

"I saw you," he said.

I waited some more.

"I couldn't believe it. Alton Wright's Hummer, that was so cool."

"You saw?"

"I was sitting right across the Pit, having a smoke. I see you and that scrawny what's-his-name get out of the Hummer and, y'know, I was thinking I had me some good weed, but not *hallucinating* good, and then you went and sank yourself. Laughed my ass off. Surprised you guys didn't hear me."

"I was sort of busy trying not to drown."

"Yeah, no shit."

We sat for a few seconds without talking, me trying to figure out how to keep Deke from telling everybody what he'd seen, and worrying about it getting back to Alton Wright.

Deke said, "I got busted for auto theft last year, y'know."

"You did?"

"Yeah. That's how come you didn't see me around school." He leaned toward me and lowered his voice. "Actually, me and Marsh, we were going for fifty, like in *Gone in Sixty Seconds*. You ever see that?"

"Yeah," I said. "It was stupid."

"No shit. But it was cool too. Anyway, Marsh and me got cracked on number fourteen. Both of us."

"You stole fourteen cars?"

He put his hand over his heart. "I swear. Only I had to give it up."

I waited.

"On account of I just turned eighteen. I got off with sixty days in juvie, plus probation, which I'm still on. That's how come I'm working here now. Got to stay employed, be a productive member of society. I get nailed again, I'm screwed." He stood up. "I'm going for another slice. Want one?"

"I'll take a Coke," I said. I watched him saunter over to the Sbarro counter, walking like he knew I was watching him, which I was. I may not have mentioned that despite his ridiculous name and tough-guy attitude and retro-thug clothing, Deke was kind of okay-looking. Not that I was interested, but at least it wasn't hard to look at him like it was with Marsh and a lot of other guys. Plus I wanted to know more about the car thing. I knew Deke had been in trouble the year before, but I hadn't realized it was for auto theft. I'd figured it was more like vandalism or stealing garden gnomes. Knowing that he was a genuine criminal type made me trust him more. I know that sounds stupid, but I figured if he was a career criminal he'd be less likely to rat me out to Alton Wright or the police.

When he returned with my Coke and another slice for himself, I asked him straight out, "You aren't going to say anything to Alton about me and his Hummer, are you?"

"Alton Wright is a rich piece of shit." He looked me in the eye then, completely serious. "I think you should steal his new FJ and see if it floats."

It wasn't exactly I-swear-on-all-that-is-holy-I-will-never-tell, but it was something, his letting me know we were on the same team.

I felt myself relax, just a little.

He said, "Y'know, what I said yesterday? I was serious. About making some money?"

I didn't say anything.

"Look, you get caught doing something when you're underage, they don't do shit."

"They locked you up for two months."

"Yeah, but I already had a record. Plus, you're a girl. Girls always get off easy."

I sat back and crossed my arms and looked at him. "You think I should become a professional car thief?"

"I'm just saying you could make some money if you wanted. I still got the connections. I just can't get caught behind the wheel. I —" He sat up straight. "Shit, my break's been over for like three minutes." He stood up and picked up an apron he'd been sitting on and a crushed paper cap. He punched the cap back into shape. Printed on the front were the words WOK ON THE WILD SIDE. With an embarrassed smile and a shrug, he put the cap on his head and tied on the apron. "Probation," he said, and walked quickly across the food court to Wing's Wild Wok.

Two things I want to make clear. I did not have any sort of a thing for Deke Moffet. His first and last names alone were enough to rule that out.

The other thing is that I was *not* seriously considering

taking up car theft as a part-time job. The fact that I had — technically — stolen four cars recently was purely a matter of irresistible opportunity, dire necessity, or peer pressure. I mean, twice it hadn't even been my idea. So the thought that I would perform grand theft auto for money was completely ridiculous.

But I have to admit I was kind of flattered that he thought I could do it.

As soon as I got outside the mall, Deke Moffet left my mind and was replaced by Jim Vail. I kept thinking how if my grandmother hadn't died, I would have been the one up in Taylors Falls fighting off his drunken advances. Or maybe if it had been me, Jim wouldn't have gotten so drunk. Or maybe I wouldn't have fought him off. The point being that if it had been me instead of Jen, things would probably have gone differently. And if they *hadn't* — if it had been *me* stuck in Taylors Falls in the middle of the night and I'd called Jen all teary and desperate — there's no way she would have stolen a car to come get me. And now, since Jim had abandoned her in the wilderness, there was no way I, her best friend, could have anything to do with him, which made me kind of mad.

As I waited for the bus to pick me up from the mall, I let my righteous anger build — not against Jim, but against Jen. I decided she was out to ruin my life, and I decided to confront her. By the time the bus arrived, I had rehearsed several versions of a conversation that would cause Jen to sob hysterically and beg my forgiveness. I imagined going to her house and barging into her room and blasting her with accusations.

Instead, I went over to Will's.

Will was the middle kid of five, with two older sisters and two younger brothers. His grandmother lived with them too, so there were like eight people in this little three-bedroom rambler. Will lived in the basement, but when I got there he was out in the backyard kicking a soccer ball with his brother Bobby.

"Hey," Will said when he saw me. He kicked the ball my way. I made a passable block and tried to kick it to Bobby, but I was off by about ten feet.

"Sorry," I called after him as he chased down the ball.

"'Sup?" Will asked.

Bobby kicked the ball to Will, who grabbed it out of the air with his hands and held on to it. I could see the disappointment on Bobby's face. My arrival had interrupted his quality time with big brother.

"I talked to Deke," I said.

Will looked away. I wondered what it was like for a boy to get pantsed in public.

I went on. "He was there at the Pit that night, smoking

dope and watching us almost get drowned. That's how he knew. But I don't think he's going to tell anybody. He doesn't like Alton much either."

"He's such a jerk," Will said.

I didn't know if he was talking about Deke or Alton. Probably both. I wanted to tell Will about Deke getting caught stealing his fourteenth car and about him suggesting that I get into the auto theft business, but I didn't because Deke and I had this unspoken agreement now. We were criminals together, and even though Will had been in on the Hummer thing, it just wasn't the same.

I said, "I'm mad at Jen."

That caught him by surprise. "Why?"

I realized then that I couldn't really talk about that either, because I couldn't tell my sort-of boyfriend Will about Jim Vail, and I also couldn't tell him about stealing the Hallsteds' Cadillac, because that would lead right back to why Jen was stuck in Taylors Falls in the middle of the night. Besides, I did not want Will to think of me as a car thief any more than he already did.

"It's a girl thing," I told him.

"Jen's nice," Will said.

"I know. I'm just being a bitch." I shrugged. "You find a dead rat yet?"

"Huh?"

"You know. To hide in Alton's new car."

"Oh. No."

"I bet you could find one over by the grain elevators. They must have lots of rats. I think they poison them."

"I'm not really so into the rat thing anymore. Even if I did it, it wouldn't change anything. Alton would still be an ass."

"You sound like my mom."

"Your mom's nice."

It was true. My mom *is* nice.

How nice my mom is:

1. When Mrs. Hallsted went to visit her sister in England, my mom invited Mr. Hallsted to have dinner with us every night for a week because she knew he didn't cook.

2. Whenever she sees a guy standing on a corner with a sign asking for money, she gives him a dollar.

3. Every year on my birthday she makes shrimp scampi and red velvet cake, my two all-time favorite foods.

4. When Jen or Will come over she always makes us some sort of snack.

5. She never forgets to send a thank-you note, even when she doesn't actually feel thankful.

6. If you have ever exchanged more than one sentence with her you will get a Christmas card.

7. She irons my T-shirts.

There's more, but you get the idea. My mother has dedicated her life to being a nice person. Now, you might be thinking that she must have a not-nice side, but you would be wrong. All of my mother's sides are nice, which puts a lot of pressure on a person like me, who can be sort of nasty, even to her friends.

I did not call Jen back for two days, even though she kept texting me. That might seem cruel, but the thing was, I knew if I talked to her I'd say something really nasty. But after two days I was feeling guilty for being mad at her so I called her and said (like nothing was ever wrong), "Let's go check out the shoe situation at DSW." Jen is crazy for shoes.

"How come you haven't called me?" she whined.

I told her my phone was messed up. I'm pretty sure she knew I was lying.

Designer Shoe Warehouse, by the way, is one of the worst places to buy shoes. They mostly deal in shoes nobody bought at full price because they're ugly. But it is also the very *best* place to buy shoes, because it's self-service and you can try on a hundred pairs and nobody makes you feel guilty for trying on too-small sizes, or not buying anything, or not putting socks on, and it's mostly free because you hardly ever find anything you want to buy. So in a way it's the perfect shoe-shopping experience if you don't actually need new shoes.

Will thinks it's ridiculous that Jen and I like to shop when we are not planning to buy anything. He calls it "air shopping." But what he doesn't get is that we just *might* buy something — and *that's* what keeps it interesting. Every now and then DSW will have the perfect pair of shoes in the right size and color and price. I bought my high-heeled strappies there. If I ever go to a formal I will have to learn how to walk in them.

Jen said she was looking for some boots for fall.

"Like elf boots," she said.

I knew exactly what she meant: pointy toes, soft floppy leather around the ankles, low heels, but not too low. I figured her chances of finding such a thing at DSW were about as good as her chances of riding her bicycle to the moon. But like I said before, that was just fine.

Me, I was hoping to find some black suede faux-athletic shoes, preferably with no stripes. Not likely, but then I didn't have any money anyway, having invested heavily in important items such as Phrap-o-chinos, fast food, and cell phone bills.

I could hardly imagine how I'd ever be able to afford a car. I mean, a car of my own.

How I get money: My father gives it to me.

He gives me an allowance of two hundred dollars a month, which is not as much as it seems like because half of it goes into a savings account for college. It used to be that *all* my money went into the college savings account. My parents opened it when I was practically a baby and put in a hundred dollars a month. When I was thirteen and started needing money desperately, my dad agreed to increase his contribution to my future. I now have more than twenty thousand dollars I can't touch and a hundred bucks a month that I usually spend in like five days.

I had made several attempts to negotiate my allowance upward. I even threatened to get a part-time job, which would probably interfere with my schoolwork. My dad called my bluff and said he thought it was a good idea, so I went out and applied for jobs at Macy's, Starbucks, and Jamba Juice. Macy's and Starbucks said no. The guy at Jamba Juice offered me a job, but the hours sucked and it was very minimum-wageish, so I decided to make do with my hundred a month plus the birthday money I always got from Grandpa John and a few other little driblets of cash like from selling my old bicycle to Jamie Weiss and emergency babysitting for my aunt Tessa's two preschoolers, which was not worth the money but I kind of had to do it.

Basically I was trying to live on about fifteen hundred dollars a year, which is pretty pathetic. It made me wonder how much a good car thief made. I would have to ask Deke if I ever ran into him again. Just out of curiosity, of course.

The thing about shopping is that even if you shop with no intention of buying anything at all, it is nice to have money so that you know if you happen to come across some amazing bargain or the perfect pair of shoes, you can buy if you want. But with only three dollars in my purse, I was not having much fun at DSW.

Jen was trying on everything in the store. I hadn't said anything to her about how I was mad at her because every time my mouth wanted to bring it up it sounded really lame. I mean, except for screaming in my ear she hadn't actually done anything *wrong*. So I just moped around the store, trying on shoes I hated, and some I didn't hate but couldn't afford, while Jen went up and down the aisles as if she was training for the Olympics speed-shopping event.

And guess what. She found her elf boots. In the one-of-a-kind clearance racks. They were pearl gray, her third-favorite color. Marked down 70 percent to $38.99.

They fit her perfectly.

"It's a miracle," she said.

I was raging jealous, especially when she paid for them with her mom's credit card. I might have said something nasty if I could have thought of anything, but I was rendered speechless by the unfairness of it all. Then Jen took me out to Sammy Wong's for spring rolls and firecracker shrimp — also on her mom's card. I couldn't stay mad at her.

I am such a total bitch inside for some reason, even though mostly I don't show it. But the things I think —

sometimes I'm surprised they don't just claw their way out through my skin.

Walking home from the bus stop, I saw Jim Vail. He was running down the sidewalk — running as in exercising — but he stopped when he saw it was me.

"Hey. Kelleigh Monahan," he said, dripping sweat and trying to control his breathing.

"Hi," I said. "How was Taylors Falls?"

"Fun!" He dragged a sweaty hand across his sweaty brow. "Only we lost Jen." He laughed weakly. "I suppose you heard about that?"

"Yeah, I had to go pick her up."

"Oh. So she's okay and everything?" I couldn't tell if he was embarrassed or not because he was already red in the face from running.

I was thinking, *Why didn't you call her to find out?* But I didn't say that. I didn't really want him to call her, because if he was a nasty drunken almost-rapist I didn't want him anywhere near my best friend . . . unless it had just been a misunderstanding and he was really a nice guy like I'd thought before. Then maybe I wanted him for myself. Someday.

"She's fine," I said.

"We're selling the puppies this week," he said. "You still want one?"

"You mean *buy* one?"

"Sure — what did you think? They're worth four hundred bucks each."

"I don't think I can afford it," I said. Not that it made any difference, since there was no way I could bring a dog home, but it bugged me that he didn't offer to give me one for free, especially since I distinctly remembered him offering me one. At least I thought at the time that was what he meant. Maybe if his mom hadn't yelled down the stairs the dog would have been for free. Even though there was no way I could have taken it.

"I think my dad would sell you Limpy for less."

Limpy was the one with the crooked foot.

"No thank you," I said.

I had been looking at the photo of my grandma Kate a lot. I tried to imagine Grandpa John holding the camera and saying "Smile!" But the girl in the photo had only a sleepy half smile. You could see a little of her teeth, bright white against her dark lips and tanned skin.

Her cutoff jeans were tight and frayed, and she had a pale L-shaped scar on her right thigh. Or it might have been a birthmark. Her halter top looked like a T-shirt that she had taken scissors to. Kate — her name had been Kate Unger back then — had probably left her home in Michigan wearing jeans and a T-shirt, and maybe a jacket, but by the time she met Grandpa John in Monterey she'd cut off and thrown away half her clothes. She had been just seventeen — I looked up her birth date and figured it out — seventeen years old on May 10, 1967. She'd taken off for California the summer after her junior year.

In the photo she looked much older than seventeen and very erotic, like maybe right after Grandpa John snapped the picture they'd had sex right there in the middle of the day on the beach.

The Volkswagen in the picture was faded green — or maybe pink, or pinkish green, if there is such a color — with a yellow hood. I wasn't sure if the two-tone effect was intentional, or if it was a junkyard patch job, or even if it was their car. The words in the margin of the photo — *Kate - Venice Beach - 1967* — were maddening in that they did not give the month. The photo could have been taken anytime after the Monterey Pop Festival, which was in June — I looked that up too. My dad was born April 17, 1968, so Kate must have gotten pregnant in July. But when *exactly* had the photo been taken?

It was driving me crazy.

I realized as I was dialing that I had never called Grandpa John on the phone before. I think that was because I was afraid Grandma Kate would answer and I'd have to listen to her raspy, whispery whining. I know that makes me a bad grandkid. I was so bad I was even a little bit glad she was gone. But I would have loved to have met the girl in the photo.

"Hello?" Grandpa John sounded angry.

"Grandpa? It's me, Kelleigh."

"Kelleigh!" His voice changed. "Is everything okay?"

"Everything's fine. How are you?"

"Staying busy. That's what they tell me I should be doing. I was just boxing up some of Kate's clothes. I don't suppose you'd be interested in going through them?"

"Uh, sure. . . ." I imagined box after box of saggy old-lady clothes. And then I imagined a pair of cutoff denim shorts. She might have saved them. Grandma Kate had been a little pack-rattish. "Yeah, I'd like that."

"I'll set 'em aside for you. Anything you don't want, which I imagine will be most of it, I'll give to the church ladies for their sale. When are you coming up for a visit?"

"I don't know. Dad's been sort of busy trying to get this rapist out of jail."

Grandpa John bellowed laughter. "Who'da thought a couple of peacenik hippies would end up raising a kid like that!"

For a second I wasn't sure if he was talking about me or my dad; then I figured out that it was Grandpa John and Kate who were the "peacenik hippies."

"You going to law school too, Kelleigh?"

"Actually, I'm thinking of becoming a criminal. To give the lawyers something to do."

He laughed again.

"Hey, thanks for sending me that picture," I said.

"Your grandmother would've wanted you to have it."

I was holding the picture in my lap.

"What about you? Do you want me to scan it for you?"

"I have lots of other pictures," he said.

"When was this one taken?" I asked.

"Nineteen sixty-seven."

"I know, but what month?"

"Um, we were in L.A., so I guess it must have been summer. Maybe July? I think by August we were back in the Bay Area."

"Was Grandma pregnant then? When you took the picture?"

It took him a few seconds to answer.

"I swear, the world went to hell the day we taught you kids to read a calendar." He paused for a breath or two, then continued. "My guess is, it was right around that time. But we didn't know it until later, of course. We were staying with this band up in San Francisco and she realized she was a month late."

"So you got married?"

"Well, we waited a few months."

"And lived happily ever after."

"Yep. Why? You aren't pregnant, are you?"

"Grandpa! No!" I felt my cheeks get hot.

"Good. You stay that way."

Desperate for a change of subject, I said, "The Volkswagen in the photo — what color is it?"

"You're the one looking at the photo, kiddo."

"I'm color-blind," I reminded him. Or maybe he never knew.

"Oh! Well, as I recall, it was faded-out red, with a yellow hood. At least that's what Kate told me. I'm color-blind too, you know."

"Was it yours or Grandma's?"

He cleared his throat and chuckled. "Kate had the VW when I met her, but it belonged to this other guy she'd been with. . . ." He trailed off the way adults do when they catch themselves talking to a kid like an adult.

I said, "Like, her boyfriend before you?"

"Something like that." He chuckled again. "Crazy times. They'd split up just before I met her, and I guess — well, you knew your grandmother. She was feisty."

I remembered her mostly as whiny. But I didn't say that.

"I didn't find out until later that she'd just gone and taken the guy's car when they broke up. I didn't know about it until he caught up with us in Santa Rosa and took it back."

"Grandma was a car thief?"

"Just that one time," he said.

––––––––

Most people think of car thieves as squinty-eyed young guys with tattoos and grease under their fingernails, but you never know who will steal a car.

––––––––

The fact that auto thievery might be as genetic as color blindness was both disturbing and reassuring. I couldn't resist asking my dad that night at dinner if he'd ever stolen a car.

He almost dropped his fork. "Have I ever *what*?" he said.

"You know, when you were young. During those wild years you never talk about."

My mother stifled a laugh with her napkin.

"I had no wild years," said my dad.

I looked at my mom, who shrugged and said, "It's true."

"I talked to Grandpa John this afternoon — he sent me that picture? Of Grandma standing in front of a VW?"

My dad nodded. "The one he kept on his desk."

"Did you know she was pregnant then?"

He blinked. "I guess I never thought about it, but I suppose she was."

"So Grandma and Grandpa had this wild hippie free-love thing going on, and you never got in trouble the whole time you were growing up?"

"Of course I got in trouble. But I certainly never stole a car!"

"Grandma did."

"She did?" My mom had this quizzical smile. "Kate stole a car?"

"Just one," I said. "That Volkswagen."

My mom looked at my dad. "This is so much more interesting than talking about your rapist again, isn't it, dear?"

In our house my dad was supposedly in charge. He earned most of the money and he was the biggest and hairiest, but in some ways my mother was even more in charge, like a farmer poking an ox with a stick to keep him headed in the right direction. Some days she poked harder than others.

"Don't worry," my dad said. "The Dandridge case is almost over. I'm going to plead him out. Turns out his brother is his fraternal twin, not identical, so the DNA evidence is back in play. And that photo of him in the bar with the baseball game? The game was taped. It turns out he was at the bar the night *after* the rape. Elwin Dandridge has been a real disappointment to me. But I think I can get him a deal for three to five, because the DEA needs his testimony in a drug-trafficking case. I might even swing a suspended sentence with probation, if he agrees to go into treatment."

"For drugs? Or raping girls?" I asked.

"I assume both. The judge is likely to —"

My mother stood up suddenly. She picked up her plate and glass of wine and said, "I'm going to eat in the den."

We watched her go, surprised. What my mom had just done was, in her version of reality, the height of rudeness.

I thought it was cool. A good hard poke to the ox's ribs.

Deke Moffet was very regular about taking his meal breaks from Wing's Wild Wok, only this time instead of pizza he was eating a burger from McDonald's. He didn't say anything right away when I sat down. I waited.

He said, "Don't worry, I haven't told anybody about the Hummer."

"Good."

"Marsh might have, though — he never shuts up. I wouldn't worry about it. Nobody really listens to him."

I nodded.

Deke said, "That what you wanted to hear?"

"Yeah, but . . . can I ask you something?"

He took another bite out of his burger and nodded.

"When you stole all those cars, how did you do it? Break in and hot-wire them? Or what?"

"Or what," Deke said. He paused to swallow. "I wouldn't know how to hot-wire a lawn mower. Besides, the kind of cars we were stealing, you can't just cross a couple wires. We weren't looking for stuff to chop. We were after the high-buck stuff — Beamers and Benzes. Cars like that got all this antitheft stuff built in. You pretty much gotta have a key." He gave me an appraising look. "Why?"

"I was just curious. How did you get the keys?"

"I got my ways." Deke hunched close over the table and lowered his voice. "I can get a key for just about any car, anywhere." He sat back and grinned.

"Then what?"

"Then what *what*?"

"You sold the cars to somebody?"

Deke took another huge bite of his burger. I waited. One thing my dad told me once is that most people can't shut up once you get them talking about their work.

He swallowed. "I sure didn't drive 'em into no pond."

"How much did you get?"

"Depended on the car. This guy I know — my client, I guess you could say — he swaps out the VINs, replates 'em, and ships 'em out of state."

"What is 'swap out the VINs'?"

"Vehicle identification numbers. He gets a new title with a new VIN number."

"How did you get caught?"

"We got pulled over for speeding." He rolled his eyes. "That moron Marsh. We weren't even in a hurry."

Being arrested for auto theft is no doubt very traumatic, as you can go to jail for it. It is not nearly as bad as rape or murder, however.

I said earlier that the only times my mom drank too much were at Book Club and weddings. I left out this one other time: when Becca Ekman, my mom's old roommate from college, came into town from New York a couple times a year and took her out for lunch. Martinis were Becca's thing.

They always went to The Oceanaire in the Hyatt, where they ripped a new one for every guy they'd ever met — which in Becca's case, I gathered, was a lot of guys. I think my mom's job was mostly to listen. She had told me a few Becca stories, I think in hopes that I would avoid following in her best friend's footsteps.

As far as I know, Becca had never stolen a car, but if she had I would not have been surprised.

Becca always stayed at the Hyatt when she came to town, so getting back to her room after multiple martinis was not a problem. But Mom always had to take a cab home and then get a ride downtown with my dad the next morning so she could pick up her car from the hotel garage. She hates cabs.

"Cabs are dirty and you never know who's going to be driving them," she says.

Elwin Carl Dandridge was a cabdriver. I don't remember if I mentioned that before.

Since I had proven to be such an excellent designated driver in the past, Mom decided that I might like to drive her downtown, then do some shopping while she and Becca got wasted, then drive her home. This was only a couple days after my air-shopping experience at DSW. I didn't know if I was into that kind of retail masochism again.

"Shopping for what? I don't have any money."

"If you promise to keep it under three hundred dollars, you can use my credit card."

Sold.

I got back to the hotel at three-thirty, wearing a new black leather jacket. It was a ridiculously hot fashion choice for the middle of summer, but wearing it was easier than carrying it. My mom was standing outside the lobby entrance with Becca, who was smoking a cigarette. I had to admit that Becca looked cool, all fashion-model slim, blowing clouds of smoke past bright red lips, totally comfortable in a pair of heels that would have given me acrophobia.

My mom also looked good, but not as good as Becca. I

noticed that she was smoking too. I walked up to her and said, "Got a cigarette?"

She did this drunken-recognition thing that would have been comical if she hadn't been my mother, and if she hadn't started coughing violently while dropping her cigarette.

Becca said, "Cool jacket, Kell."

My mom was about as smashed as I'd ever seen her, talking fast like a meth freak and slurring her words and making hand gestures like a conductor. I was concentrating on getting off the parking ramp and out of downtown Minneapolis, so I hardly heard what she was saying — mostly *Becca said this, Becca said that, blah-blah-blah* — until we were finally on the freeway and I heard her say something about Dad.

". . . expect me to have dinner on the table as usual, he's lucky he didn't marry Becca — "

"*Dad* used to go out with *Becca*?" I said.

"Don't be silly. I'm just saying, she'd have told him where to put his dinner!" She laughed. "Your dad — " She burped and made a sour face. "Remind me to never *ever* drink another apricot martini."

"Dad what?"

"Do you know all the time he was in law school, and for the first five years of our marriage, he never once said 'I love you'? You know what he said? He said 'I *luff* you.' And every time he said it, he'd laugh. A fakey little laugh. *Huh huh.* Like a kid. 'I *luff* you, *huh huh.*' Can you imagine?"

I tried. I couldn't. My big hairy dad saying "I *luff* you"? No way.

"He says 'I love you' all the time," I said. "I've heard him say it."

"He says it *now*, but only because now it's not true. Before, it scared him because it *might* have been true. But then he just decided one day to lie, and once he decided to lie, it was easy for him to say it." She extended her fingers and stared at her nails. She'd had them done the day before, getting herself all fixed up for Becca.

My head was spinning with what she'd said. I mean, I was trying to understand it, trying to make sense of her words. Dad could only say *I love you* if it wasn't true? Did that make sense on any level other than the multiple-apricot-martini level?

My mother let her manicured hand fall to her lap.

"He does it for a living, you know," she said, sounding perfectly sober for the moment. "He tells lies."

Knowing that her martini lunch would incapacitate her, my mother had made a bean-and-lamb casserole and a salad that morning. When we got home, she put the casserole in the oven, took two Excedrin, and went to bed, asking me to wake her up at five-thirty. I went to my computer and spent the next hour on the Web.

I did a search for "how to steal a car" and got twenty thousand hits. A lot of them were videos with hot-wiring instructions. I watched a few of those. Every one was different. Some said to cross the green wire with the red; some said the red with the yellow; some said to cross all three. It looked really complicated. I could see why Deke had never learned to do it.

One video showed a guy jamming the tip of a screwdriver into the ignition switch and turning it to start the car. But if it was really that simple, then why would all these other guys bother with the hot-wiring? Another video showed a girl breaking into a locked car using nothing but a tennis ball. She cut a small hole in the tennis ball, put the hole over the lock, and smooshed the ball with her palm. The sudden air pressure made the lock pop up. Cool.

There were a few videos of guys actually stealing cars. Some of them you could tell were real — you could see how pumped they were, yelling and grinning and high-fiving each other.

I heard my mom in the shower just after five. I erased my browsing history and went downstairs to read about Ishmael and his cannibal friend, Queequeg, who is actually the coolest character in the whole book. By the time my dad got home, Mom was acting and looking almost normal, although she was moving a little slow and her eyes were red.

I decided to try an experiment.

After dinner that night, during which there was no mention of Elwin Carl Dandridge, my dad put on his suburban warrior outfit and went out to attack the bushes with his electric trimmer. I helped my mom clean up the kitchen. She was looking a bit less hollow-eyed.

"Are you hungover?" I asked.

"I'm not twenty-five anymore," she said, scraping the leftover casserole into a plastic container. "I don't know how Becca does it."

"I noticed that Dad didn't give us his usual update on his free-the-guilty-rapist program."

She laughed weakly. "I'll finish up here," she said.

I went outside and watched my dad squaring off the boxwood hedge that divides our yard from the Hallsteds', who were still up at their lake cabin.

"Hey, Dad!" I yelled it loud to get through his earmuffs.

He turned off the trimmer and pulled his earmuffs down around his neck.

"What was in that envelope?" I asked.

He looked puzzled.

"The one the police left in the Hallsteds' door," I explained. "The one I gave you last week?"

"Oh! That was just . . . apparently someone got into the Hallsteds' garage and stole their car. It was found abandoned the next day over on Dakota Avenue. As far as we can tell, they didn't break into the house. The police are keeping the car at the impound lot until the Hallsteds get back next week."

I must have looked worried, because he set his trimmer on the grass and gave me a hug. "I didn't want you to worry, Kell. It was probably just some kids. They must have used a remote to get into the garage."

I hugged him back. The hard plastic earmuffs around his neck ground into my cheek. My dad had been doing a lot of hugging the past couple of years, ever since the sensitivity training program his law firm had to go through after one of the lawyers got sued for harassment.

"You haven't seen any strangers hanging around the neighborhood, have you?" he said into my ear.

"Nope."

He released me. "Well, let me know if you do, okay?"

"I love you, Daddy."

That was my experiment.

"Me too, honey. I love you too," he said as if it was the most natural and true thing in the world.

He lifted his earmuffs onto his ears, picked up the trimmer, smiled at me, and pulled the starter cord.

I had to show Jen my new jacket, but when I called, her dad told me she had gone down to Red Wing with her mom for an overnight antiquing trip. That was Jen's mom's thing —

antiquing — and Jen had gotten dragged into it the same way I had gotten into Pilates with *my* mom, though I have to admit that sometimes she came back from these trips with some really cool stuff, like the Scooby Doo thermos she'd bought for two dollars at an estate sale. So with Jen off bonding and scavenging with her mom, I was kind of at a loss. I could show the jacket to Will but he'd be like, *Hey, cool*, which was the way he was all the time, unless his sexual preference was questioned by Alton Wright.

I wondered if Jen had told Will about the Cadillac.

I wondered if Will would think stealing the Cadillac was cool, or just stupid.

I wondered if Will really *was* gay. It would be ironic if he'd had me steal Alton's Hummer because Alton had told the truth for once. I'm not sure if *ironic* is the right word, but you get what I mean. But just because Will was not constantly trying to get naked with Jen and me did not mean he was gay. He sure didn't *seem* gay. For example, he dressed really sloppy and his preferred music was of the high-testosterone, head-banging variety. It wasn't like he was all into fashion and listening to Madonna or Cher or George Michael or something. . . . I don't know, maybe those are just stereotypes. My point is that Will did not exactly set off anybody's gaydar, but then, neither did Abraham Lincoln, and somebody once told me he was gay. It's probably not true though.

I hung the jacket over one shoulder and walked to Will's. I figured if he happened to be out in the yard or something he could tell me how cool my new jacket was or whatever, but when I got there I saw no signs of life. I kept on walking and eventually got to Charlie Bean's, but nobody I knew was there and I didn't have any money anyway, so I turned around and walked back. This time when I went by, Will was out on the driveway, shooting baskets.

"Hey," he said when he saw me. He looked at the jacket hanging on my shoulder and raised his eyebrows like, did I not know it was eighty degrees out?

"It's new," I said. "I'm breaking it in."

"Cool." He bounced the basketball onto the lawn. "I saw you earlier," he said.

"Earlier when?"

"When you walked by."

"I went up to Charlie Bean's but I didn't have any money."

"Come on," Will said, grabbing my hand. "I'll buy you a Phrap-o-whatchacallit."

It was like an electric shock when he touched me. I couldn't remember Will ever doing anything like that before. He had always been so standoffish.

The hand-holding only lasted about two seconds. As soon as we started walking, he let go and we were like before, moving along in the same direction, but with about twelve inches and my new jacket between us. I shifted the jacket to my other shoulder.

"I wanted to talk to you about something," Will said. Another shock. Will *never* wanted to talk. Ever.

He said, "I was thinking about what we did. You know, with Alton's Hummer?"

"I've been thinking about that too."

"Really?" He slowed his pace and peered at me sideways.

"Yeah . . ." I was about to say, *It was really fun!* Or *Let's do it again!* But something I saw in the set of his jaw — or maybe it was the wrinkled forehead — made me pause. Instead, I said, "That was really something," which is one thing you can say about absolutely anything.

"It was really stupid," said Will.

Ka-thunk. That wasn't what I'd been thinking at all.

Keeping my voice light, I said, "So you think the dead rat would have been more effective?"

"Equally stupid. What I wanted to say was . . . I want to apologize. We could have gotten into a lot of trouble. You could have gotten *killed*. It was like, you took that car with Jen that time? And for some stupid reason I got jealous, like you guys were having this exciting life, and at the same time I was all pissed off at Alton because of him telling everybody I was gay, and then, I don't know, I guess I wasn't thinking. We were just really lucky we didn't get caught is all."

"Or drownded," I said.

"Or drownded."

We walked up to the outside ordering window at Charlie

Bean's. Will put his hands in his pockets, then looked at me with a funny expression on his face.

"Oops," he said.

"What?"

"I forgot. I left my wallet in my other pants."

Will was the kind of guy who, when he did something like that, you didn't get mad at, even though he never actually said he was sorry. This one other time he took me and Jen out for pizza and did the same thing after we'd eaten the pizza. Jen just paid for it. It was understood that Will didn't do it because he was cheap or broke; he just wasn't thinking, and even though he didn't pay, you still liked him because he had *wanted* to pay. How a guy like that ends up with two girlfriends, I don't know. So even though I wasn't mad at him exactly, I was kind of irritated because I'd really wanted that Phrap-o-chino. So on the way back to his house, I decided to make him squirm.

"Do you like me?" I asked.

"Sure."

"How about Jen?"

"I like Jen too."

"Did Jen tell you I stole another car?"

Will stopped walking.

"Are you shitting me?"

"It was an emergency."

He waited for me to explain, but of course I couldn't, since it involved Jen going off to Taylors Falls with Jim Vail.

To change the subject quick, I said, "So, if you're not gay, how come you're not always trying to have sex with us?" I watched his face. It took a few seconds, but I could see a blush creeping up his neck.

"I don't know," he said.

"It's kind of weird. I mean, if we don't have to fight you off all the time, how do we know you really like us?"

"I don't know." He wouldn't look at me.

Funny thing: If I had thought he might say anything else, I'd never have asked the question.

I called Britt Johnson, who was friends with Deke's sister Callie, or so I thought.

"Why do you want Callie's number?" Britt asked. "She's a total skank."

"What did she do?"

"You know Aaron? She's like all over him."

"I thought you and him broke up like months ago."

"So?"

I told Britt I'd found a book with Callie's name in it and I wanted to return it.

"I'd just trash it," Britt said.

I laughed. "C'mon."

Britt said, "Whatever," and gave me Callie's home number.

Deke wasn't home but he called me back later that night. I was already in bed but I'd left my cell on just in case.

"Hey, it's me. What's up?" he said.

I told him what I wanted.

He said, "I knew you was a freak."

Several days went by and I didn't hear from Deke. I was starting to think he was full of crap just like everybody else, so I tried not to think about it. It was around then that Jen and I had a heart-to-heart over a bottle of wine she'd swiped from her parents' "wine cellar." That was what her dad called the two or three dozen bottles stacked in a corner of their basement. The wine was white and kind of sour. I don't remember what it was. It could have been worth a thousand dollars, for all I know.

Jen's parents were gone on an overnight to Chicago, so we sat in her living room and drank the wine out of their fancy wineglasses. We would have been smoking cigarettes too, except neither of us smoked.

Our heart-to-heart was mostly about Jim Vail. Jen was still messed up over what had happened, and what had *almost* happened at Taylors Falls, and about two-thirds of the way through the bottle of wine I blurted about me and Jim and the puppies and how I was mad at her for going with him, and she started crying and saying she was sorry and I started crying too, saying I knew it wasn't her fault 'cause she didn't know I had been supposed to go and I would have done the same thing except I'd probably have gotten myself raped and so actually she saved me by being the one to go, which was ridiculous, of course, because it was actually my grandmother who saved me by dying.

We also talked about Will. Jen was convinced he was either gay or a eunuch.

"He's not a eunuch," I said. "Eunuchs don't have deep voices."

"Then he must be gay."

"I think he's just shy."

Jen sipped her wine thoughtfully. "That is so sweet," she said.

We talked about other things — I don't remember what. But I never mentioned Deke Moffet.

I stayed at Jen's overnight to sleep it off. The next morning when I got home from Jen's with my head pounding and my stomach churning, my mom was all dressed in her Pilates outfit, waiting for me. I had completely forgotten about Pilates. I quick changed and in about five minutes we were out the door, with her driving. She was in a chatty mood, and I was finding out what a hangover felt like. I thought about her that night after she went out with Becca Ekman, how hard it must have been to sit at the dinner table listening to my dad talk about his day and probably wanting to puke the whole time.

Just to be perfectly clear, I am not this big-time drinker. I had drunk three times in my life and splitting that one bottle of wine with Jen was the most I'd ever had at one time. But even with my limited experience, I can offer some solid advice: Do not get drunk the night before your Pilates class.

After an hour of building my core strength (a Pilates thing) and trying to not throw up (a wine thing), I went with my mom for brunch to Chez Colette in the Sofitel hotel, way out in Bloomington. My mom had this thing for their croissants. Also, the place made her feel all French and classy.

I drank two café au laits and ate a chocolate croissant while my mother chattered on about I-don't-know-what. I finally got tired of whatever it was she was talking about and asked her how dad was doing with his rapist.

"Your father is very serious about his work, Kelleigh," she said, putting on her we-are-your-parents-and-we-are-a-team face. "He believes that every person accused of a crime deserves vigorous representation."

"Vigorous representation?"

"That's how he puts it."

"Do you think he's really going to get that guy off? Do I need to start carrying pepper spray?"

She shook her head, looking thoughtful, and said, "I don't know. With that break-in at the Hallsteds', pepper spray might not be a bad idea."

On the way to the car, my mom handed me her keys, even though all she'd been drinking was coffee. I didn't really feel like driving because I still had a headache, and driving with a parent watching your every move is not nearly as interesting as driving on your own. But it would have been weird for me not to want to drive, so I drove.

As I was crossing over the freeway to get to the eastbound entrance ramp, I saw my dad. It was just a flash. White Lexus, my dad's face through the tinted windshield, and then I was turning onto the freeway.

"I just saw Dad," I said.

My mother looked at me.

"What? Where?"

"He was going the other way."

She looked around. "Are you sure?"

"I think so."

"What on earth would he be doing way out here? His office is downtown."

I shrugged. I was already wishing I hadn't said anything.

"You must have been mistaken," she said.

"It might have just been a guy who looked like him."

"There are a lot of white Lexuses." She flipped open her cell phone, stared at it for a few seconds, shook her head slightly, closed it, and put it back in her bag.

"Be careful here," she said, pointing ahead. "The right lane is closed."

I changed lanes, signaling and checking both mirrors like you're supposed to.

"We should stop at the store," she said. "We need milk."

"Okay," I said. I did not mention that my dad had not been alone in his car. Or that the woman sitting beside him looked like a younger version of my mother.

I decided if Deke ever called I would laugh and say something like "Hey, I was just kidding. Ha-ha." That's what I thought I'd do. But then he did call. It was the same day I saw my dad with the woman by the Sofitel. And instead of saying I'd just been kidding, I said, "Okay, I'll do it." But I still didn't think I was *really* going to do it. I told myself something would happen. My other grandmother would die or there would be a tornado or something.

That night when my dad got home from work, we had BLTs and baked beans for dinner — as minimal a meal as my mother was capable of preparing. I had thought she didn't believe what I'd said about seeing Dad, but I could tell by the way she was acting that she *did* believe me. Maybe she'd seen him herself, and seen the woman in the car too, but hadn't wanted to admit it to me.

As we were eating, my dad told a long story about something that had happened to him in college but I wasn't listening. I was watching my mom. Usually she's full of questions, always keeping the conversation going. Like *And then what happened?* or *What did you have for lunch?* or *What were you doing way out by the Sofitel in the middle of the day?*

She didn't ask him anything at all, the whole meal.

I think she was afraid he would lie to her.

After dinner, my mom cleaned the kitchen in that loud, pot-banging sort of way she did when she was upset. My dad went into his study to shuffle papers around or whatever it was he did in there. I turned on the TV and watched an old *Sex and the City* rerun, except I wasn't really watching it, I was thinking about how I was going to get out of meeting Deke.

I had told him I would meet him at Charlie Bean's the next afternoon, but I'd decided I wasn't actually going to do it. The easiest thing would be to tell him I was sick, so I was trying to decide what kind of disease I should have — something that lasted a while — when the phone rang.

My dad picked up the phone in his study, and I could tell from the tone of his voice that something bad had happened.

My head went to all the usual places: another death in the family, a serious financial crisis that would force us to live on macaroni and cheese, a diagnosis of cancer or plague, a death threat from terrorist rapists — all the standard horrors. Then Sarah Jessica Parker's heel broke at exactly the most embarrassing possible moment, and my mother turned on the garbage disposal, and all the conversations with Deke I'd been rehearsing kind of smooshed together and I thought how nice it would be to be bulimic at that moment so I could go to the bathroom and puke. Instead of puking, I turned up the volume on the TV and tried hard to care about Sarah Jessica Parker's shoe crisis.

What happened: Elwin Carl Dandridge got knifed.

One of the other inmates thought that raping eight girls was sufficient cause for murder, so he stabbed him three times with the sharpened handle of a spoon. Apparently, it is not that easy to kill someone with a spoon, because instead of being dead, Dandridge was in the prison hospital. My dad felt he had to rush right over there to sit with his injured serial rapist and, I don't know, write down his dying words or something. Actually, I think he was looking for an excuse to get out of the house, what with my mom acting so weird.

He didn't get home until almost midnight. I was slouched in his recliner, reading about Captain Ahab and his leg made out of a whale's jawbone, when he walked in and told me that Elwin Carl Dandridge was going to be all right.

"His wounds were superficial. But he'll have to be placed in solitary confinement when they release him from the hospital wing."

Like it was the best thing that could possibly happen, keeping the rapist safe.

Then he asked me if Mom was still up, and I told him she'd gone to bed an hour ago. That seemed to make him happy too.

The next morning when I got up, my dad was packing his suitcase. I had this stomach-dropping moment when I thought he was moving out, like they were getting divorced or something, but he told me my mom was driving him to the airport for an overnight trip to Colorado.

"We've located a man who can alibi Elwin Dandridge for several of the alleged rapes. I've been trying to find him for the past month, and it turns out he's been in jail in Denver. I just need to get a statement from him."

"What's he in jail for?"

"Auto theft."

"Oh. Are you going to defend him too?"

"He has a lawyer. It's a first offense, so I doubt he'll do any jail time beyond the time he's already served." He shrugged. "Nobody gets too excited these days about stolen cars."

"I was sure you were going to back out," Deke said with a grin.

I sat down across from him. There were two Phrap-o-chinos sitting on the small table. His was half empty.

"But you bought me a Phrap anyways."

"Just in case."

"What if I *hadn't* shown up?"

"I'd have drunk it myself."

That wasn't exactly what I'd meant.

"How long have you been here?" I asked.

"Just a couple minutes."

I took a sip of my drink. It was warm, but not hot. I got up and went over to the station with the stir sticks and sugar and stuff, added three packets of sugar, stirred it in, and went back to the table.

He watched me take another sip, then said, "So . . . you really up for this?"

I'd always thought that stealing cars was something you did at night, but according to Deke, the best time is in the middle of the day, and the best place is in a big busy parking lot, like at a mall where nobody pays any attention to just another teenager.

"Best part is you just have to drive it about a mile to the Park & Ride and leave it there."

I didn't get it. "What's the point?" I asked.

"To make sure it doesn't have a transmitter on it," he said.

"What's that?"

"You know — those signal things they put in some cars so if they get stolen the cops can locate them. We drop the car at the Park & Ride, and if no cops show up, my guy has one of his guys pick it up the next morning."

"So all I have to do is drive the car a mile and I get a thousand dollars?"

"Minus for the key. Minus my cut for setting it up."

"Leaving what?"

"Two-fifty?"

I laughed. "How about five hundred?"

"It's only like two minutes of work!" he said.

"Yeah, and I risk getting caught and going to jail."

"Look, I have to deal with the guy, then locate a car like what he wants, then get the VIN number so I can order a key, and pay the key guy — five hundred bucks just for the key! Then I got to follow the guy whose car it is to work or whatever so we know the best time and place to grab the car, and then deal with you, and —"

"Okay, okay," I said. "I'll do it for two-fifty."

"And you won't go to jail, because you've got a clean record and you're only sixteen."

I corrected him. "Fifteen."

His eyes widened. "You don't have a license?"

I started laughing at the expression on his face, then he was laughing too because if I got pulled over, not having a license would be the least of my problems.

You hear a lot about car thieves hot-wiring cars, but it is much easier to use a key. That way you don't have to damage the car. Also, many new cars are equipped with antitheft devices that make hot-wiring impossible, or they might have transmitters so the police can track them down by following a signal. To get around that, the thief must park the car in a safe place for a day or two to let it "cool down."

I should say something about my mental state during all this: Happy and Relaxed.

I think it was the rules. There was no fuzziness about what Deke and I were doing. It was immoral, illegal, risky, and entertaining. I was not distracted by thoughts of Jen or Will or Jim Vail or Elwin Carl Dandridge or even, in a way, Deke Moffet. Because Deke was not really Deke the Boy — he was more like Deke the Auto Thief. He was not who he *was* — he was what he *did*. Like we each had a job to do, and until the job was over we were defined by what we did. What we had to do. I think this is why guys like football, and why they join the army, because as long as you are playing the game or following orders you do not have to figure out who you really are.

Deke had a little blue pickup truck that he actually owned. It was a mess, with a bunch of McDonald's wrappers and cups on the floor, and it reeked of cigarettes.

"You smoke?" I asked.

"Marsh does."

"Oh." I had been wondering about Marshall Cassidy. "Before, you were boosting cars with Marshall. How come now you're doing it with me?"

"Marsh is sort of . . . unreliable. If it wasn't for him we'd never have gotten caught. It was really stupid. Both of us in the car — I mean, what was the point? We should have just taken turns. Why risk both of us getting cracked? Plus he was driving fifty in a thirty zone and got us pulled over. I should've known better than to let him drive. He'd been smokin' bathtub."

"What's that?"

"It's this cheap meth."

Meth. That made perfect sense. Marshall Cassidy was one of those guys just born to be a meth freak.

"But you guys are still friends?"

"Marsh and me, we been tight since we were like five."

Just like me and Jen.

Deke turned off I-394 onto Ridgedale Drive, then into the parking lot on the Macy's side of Ridgedale Center. He drove up and down the rows of cars, then stopped.

"There it is," he said, pointing. "The silver Benz."

He showed me a thing that looked like a small cell phone.

"This car has what you call a keyless option. You just put this thing — I guess it's a keyless key — you put it in your pocket, and when you walk up to the car it automatically unlocks the doors. You get in, put your foot on the brake, press the start button on the dash, and take off. Nice and slow — nobody's gonna be chasing you."

I took the key.

"Now you go shopping," he said.

"You mean *car* shopping?" I said, thinking he was making a dumb joke.

"No. Go into Macy's and look at some stuff, then walk out the other entrance so it looks like you're coming out of the mall and going to your car. That way nobody connects you with me."

"Thanks a lot."

"You know what I mean."

"Fine." I put on my sunglasses, got out of the truck, headed into Macy's, and walked through the men's department, then into the mall and out the mall entrance past the bench where Jen and I had been sitting the day I'd seen the guy drop his car keys. I reached into my purse and felt around. The Nissan keys were still there, way down in the bottom. I could feel the Mercedes key in my jeans pocket, almost like it was hot. I stood there on the curb for what seemed like a long time, then something inside me clicked, and I stepped off the curb and headed diagonally across the parking lot toward it, my heart pounding harder and faster with every step.

I was opening the Mercedes door when I heard someone say, "Hey!"

I froze.

"Cordelia?"

I turned toward the voice. A guy — tall, a few years older than me with dark hair and close-set features — smiling. He had on a pair of those jeans that underpaid Asians spend hours beating the crap out of just to make them look old, even though you can tell right away they're fake.

I said, "Ummm . . ." And then it hit me who he was. Only I couldn't remember his name.

"Tyler," he said. "From the Minnehaha Club pool? You're Cordelia, right?"

I remembered I had told him my name was Cordelia.

"You guys never showed up," I said. "At the Starbucks?"

"Oh! Uh, we didn't think *you'd* show up." He ran his eyes over the car the same way he'd looked at me in my bathing suit.

"Nice ride," he said.

"It's my boyfriend's."

"Cool. So, what's going on?"

"Nothing?" I said. Looking past him I could see Deke in his truck, gesticulating. "Listen, I gotta get going," I said.

He looked disappointed. "Okay. Well. It was good to see you."

"Good to see you," I said. I got into the car and closed the door.

The inside of a Mercedes-Benz is so quiet it feels at first as if your ears have stopped working. I found the start button on the dash next to the steering wheel and pressed it. The dashboard display lit up, but the car didn't start. Tyler was still standing a few feet away, watching me and smiling. I pressed the button again. Nothing. Tyler was still watching me, and I had a sudden panic attack. *What if this is his car?* But he looked too calm for that. I remembered then that Deke had said something about the brake, so I put my foot on the brake pedal and pressed the start button again.

The engine started with a deep hum, and the car began beeping loudly. The panicky feeling got worse for a second, until I figured out what it was. I fastened the seat belt and the beeping stopped.

I put the car in gear. As soon as it started moving, my panic went away. I felt like I was in a dream. I drove out of the parking lot, around the entire mall, then re-entered the lot by Macy's. Tyler was nowhere in sight. I parked the car in the exact same spot and walked away from it. I was almost back to the sidewalk in front of Macy's when Deke pulled up in his pickup.

"What the hell?" he said.

I got in beside him.

"I'm sorry," I said.

Deke said, "Look, you said he doesn't even know your real name."

"He could find out."

"Why would he?"

"I'm irresistible?"

"Seriously, he's not even going to remember he talked to you. I know guys like that. You're just another girl to him."

"He was really interested in the car. And he remembered my name."

"Your *fake* name. Besides, what are the chances he ever finds out that the car he saw you get into was stolen? Cars get boosted every day. You ever see anything about it in the news? Hell no. Unless somebody gets jacked with a baby in the backseat or something. It's what they call a victimless crime — except for the insurance company, and nobody cares about them. Besides, even if he did remember and found out who you are and all, nobody would believe him. Girls don't steal cars, they —"

"Shut up," I said. Or maybe shouted. I opened the door and got out and slammed it.

Deke rolled the window down and kept talking, getting mad now. "I paid five hundred bucks for that key!"

"So do it yourself!"

"I will if I have to. Gimme the key." He leaned across the seat and stuck his hand out the open window. I took the key out of my pocket and looked at it. My heart was going crazy again and I felt like I couldn't get enough air. I backed away from him, then ran over to the Mercedes, got in, and slammed the door.

Silence.

I pressed the start button.

Nobody in the history of driving ever drove better than I drove that eight-tenths of a mile from the Macy's parking lot to the Park & Ride. Each second stretched out to a minute as I used every ounce of concentration to bring utter flawlessness to my performance. I imagined my dad, my mom, Deke Moffet, Will, the faceless man who would one day give me my driver's test, and God all watching my every move. I did not disappoint them. I was perfect.

———

Afterward when he picked me up just down the street from the Park & Ride, Deke said, "You did good."

"Thanks." I had this buzzy, hollow feeling inside, like I had done something really important. Not necessarily something good, but something real.

"Let's go over to the Pit and smoke a bowl," he said. "Celebrate."

"No thanks." The last thing I wanted was to sit next to a stinky pond and fry my brain cells. I wanted to hang on to that buzzy feeling, but not the kind of buzz Deke was talking about.

"You don't smoke?"

"I think I just want to go home," I said.

That night we had a quiet dinner, just me and my mom eating crunchy BLTs and tomato soup. Neither of us had much to say. I wondered what was going on in her head, but mostly I was thinking about what was going on in *my* head. My drive from the parking lot to the Park & Ride kept playing in my head like a loop, over and over.

Later I went to my room and tried to read some more *Moby-Dick*, but the words started looking like little black squiggles, and then I must have fallen asleep, because when I woke up I was still dressed and my alarm clock read 5:13 a.m.

I got up and, without even changing my clothes, I walked

all the way to the Park & Ride, which took almost an hour. The Mercedes was still parked where I'd left it. I turned around.

When I got home, my mom was making french toast.

"*You* got up early," she said.

Jen called just as I was about to call Deke, who told me never to call him before ten, so I talked to her for a while. She was on a rant about Will, who had gone to the pool with her, and instead of hanging out with her, had started talking to these guys.

"Remember the blond guy? What's his name? Damien?"

"Or Andre."

"Yeah. They know each other. I guess he works at Ducky's sometimes and they're both into, I don't know, some sort of gaming thing. So I . . ."

I just wanted to call Deke, and I was trying to figure out if there was a way you could text somebody in the middle of a call to somebody else, and Jen just kept chattering until finally I told her my mom was calling me. When I hung up, I had this moment of confusion over why Jen and I were such good friends.

Deke wasn't home, but I got him on his cell.

"It's still there," he told me. "I just drove past it. They should have picked it up by now. Let me call you back."

A few minutes later my cell rang.

"Neal said the cops were watching it all night," Deke said.

"Who's Neal?"

"The guy who isn't going to be paying us any money on account of the car's got a transmitter on it."

"Oh." The fragment of buzz I still had left whooshed out of me. "Now what?"

"Now I'm out five hundred bucks, and Neal's pissed. We have to find another Benz."

I didn't say anything. I was thinking about the car sitting in the Park & Ride with some undercover cop watching it through big official-looking binoculars, just waiting to pounce. Would they take my fingerprints from the steering wheel? Would Tyler the pool guy hear about it and report me? Did anybody else see me?

"You up for it?" he asked.

"I don't know," I said. I really didn't.

Jen was still upset about the Will thing when I got back to her later that afternoon. She wanted me to come over, so I said okay and talked my mom into dropping me off at Jen's on her way to a church meeting. When Jen opened the door, I knew in one second she was drunk.

"My parents are up at Izatys for the weekend," she said. "I think they go there so they can do it."

"They can't do it here?"

"My presence inhibits them."

"They *told* you that?"

"You know how weird they are about sex."

"Oh." Sometimes I forget about what happened to Jen when she was eleven.

What happened to Jen when she was eleven: Her sixteen-year-old cousin was staying with them because he'd been kicked out of school in Des Moines for smoking dope, and his mom, Jen's mom's sister, didn't know what to do with him. So he stayed a month at Jen's and she really liked him at first, until he started visiting her room at night. She let it go on for a couple of weeks before telling her mom. So technically Jen is not a virgin, but officially she still is one because, when you're only eleven, it shouldn't count.

Jen and I were already best friends back then, but she never said a word to me about her cousin and what he did until three years later when her therapist told her she should talk about it. And right after she told me all about it she said she never wanted to talk about it again, so we never did. But sometimes we would talk about other things and what we said wouldn't make any sense except for us both knowing what happened with her cousin. Like she would tell me how if she was watching TV with her parents and a sex scene came on, they would start talking really loud about ice cream or something. Anything about sex made them act weird, according to Jen, but that was fine with her. She once told me that when she was a little kid she would hear them doing it in their bedroom and she would think they were hurting each other. After the thing with her cousin, they stopped doing it where she could hear them, or if they did they were really quiet.

Most of the time Jen was perfectly normal. I didn't think about her as a girl who had been molested. It was so long ago. But I know that things that happen when you're a little kid can mess you up pretty good inside. I guess it can mess up your parents too.

"I am so pissed at Will," Jen said, pouring herself another glass of red wine. "You want some?" The bottle was almost empty.

"No thanks," I said. I remembered all too clearly my recent hangover.

She tipped the rest of the wine into her glass and took a big sip. She was sitting on the beige sofa. I couldn't believe she hadn't spilled on it yet, the way she was holding the glass all crooked and everything.

"I think you're right," she said. "Will is gay."

"I never said he was gay."

"You said he might be."

"I don't remember what I said, but I don't think I said he's gay."

"Why not?"

I wasn't sure why not — maybe Will *was* gay — but Jen was bugging me with all her drunken whining. It is definitely no fun to be not-drunk with someone who is way-drunk.

Jen said, "So this guy Andre or Damien or whatever works weekends at the car wash, and he and Will are both into some stupid video game and they're talking some weird video game language, and I'm like, *Hello?* I think they're *both* gay."

I wanted to say, *So what if they are? I stole another car.* But I didn't.

". . . and I wanted to play mini golf, but Will kept saying 'Just a minute,' and finally I went up to the sundeck and when I came down later, they were gone. He was supposed to be my *guest*."

I wanted to say, *Do you have any idea how trivial and boring this is? Do you realize that I stole another car?* But I didn't.

"I think we should break up with him," Jen said. She grabbed my wrist and got right in my face and said, "You have to swear you'll break up with him too."

"Okay," I said, mostly so she would stop breathing wine breath on me.

Jen burst into alcoholic tears, and the funny thing was, I sat there and watched her and I didn't feel bad for her or anything, just sort of mildly disgusted, like if I'd noticed a stain on her sofa after all.

When I got home, my mom was in the kitchen talking on the phone all cheerful to one of her charities and fussing over a roast. It was a big piece of meat, which meant that she expected Dad to get home from Colorado in time for dinner. I grabbed a juice box from the fridge and started up to my room, but I'd only gotten as far as the stairs when she called me back, holding her hand over the mouthpiece of the phone, smiling the way she does when she needs a favor.

"Sweetie, your dad's plane will be in at four-thirty and I'm going to have to leave in a minute to pick him up. Can you watch the roast?"

"You mean like just sit there and *watch* it?"

"No, I —" She remembered she was on the phone. "Betty? Can I call you back? Thanks. Let's talk tomorrow." She hung up. "That was Elizabeth Crowe from the MS Society. Oh my God, you can't believe what's going on there — oh! Look at the time! Where's my purse?"

Like I cared. But I did think it was interesting how bright and chatty and wild-eyed my mom was. Then I noticed the half-empty glass of white wine on the counter, a very odd thing, as my mother never drank except for one glass at dinner and on special occasions like Book Club, or with Becca. She was looking for her purse and telling me how I had to turn the roast once at forty-five minutes and turn it off at one hour twenty minutes in case she didn't get back, and would I also make a green salad and set the table, please? I saw the wine bottle over by the stove about three quarters empty. At least she wasn't as drunk as Jen, but what was going on here anyway? Everybody I knew was all of a sudden drinking in the middle of the day. Would my dad be loaded on scotch from the airplane?

"Why don't you let me drive?" I said, holding up the depleted wine bottle.

My mom's face fell, then instantly brightened. "Oh, sweetie, I used most of that for the marinade."

"I've driven to the airport before," I said.

"But who will watch the roast?"

"Why don't you stay here and I'll go get Dad."

"Kelleigh! You don't even have your license!"

"I'll be legal to drive on the way home, because Dad will be in the car."

"You're being ridiculous."

"Yeah, and *you're* being drunk."

"I am *not* drunk!"

Eventually she decided to turn the oven to low and let me drive both of us to the airport. But as we were getting into the car, she threw her hands up like she was scattering confetti and said, "Oh, this is silly. You're a good driver. You go. He'll be waiting at the far end of the baggage claim level. I'll stay and get dinner ready. Just don't get pulled over."

That just goes to show how alcohol can lead to bad parenting decisions.

My dad was waiting at the curb with his overnight bag.

"Where's your mother?" was the first thing out of his mouth.

"She was having a crisis," I said. "She said it would be okay for me to drive here alone."

He stared at me. I could almost hear the lawyerly wheels turning in his head.

"What sort of crisis?"

"Cooking-related," I said.

He threw his bag into the backseat, walked around the car, and opened the driver's-side door.

"I'm driving," he said.

On the way home, he seemed tense and distracted. I guessed his interview with the auto thief hadn't gone the way he'd hoped. When we got home, the wine bottle was nowhere in sight. Mom had changed her top and put on fresh makeup, and she was drinking iced tea. I watched them do their kiss/hug/kiss/hug thing, only it was more like they were going through the motions than like they wanted to touch each other, and I got this déjà vu feeling like we'd been through all this before.

My father's first affair happened when I was in third grade.

At the time, I didn't know what was going on, only that my parents were acting all stiff and weird and having lots of long conversations in their bedroom with the door closed. I remember that time like a dream or the way you remember being really sick. I think it only lasted a few weeks and then slowly everybody started acting normal again, but it felt like months. It was the first time I'd ever imagined the possibility that our family might fly to pieces, and it scared me worse than anything.

The short version that I eventually pieced together from eavesdropping on some of my mom's phone calls was that my dad had an affair with one of his clients, and my mom found out about it. For a while it looked like they might get divorced, but after going to counseling they figured things out and everything was sort of okay again.

I don't think either of them knew how much it messed me up knowing that something had gone horribly wrong, even though I didn't understand at the time what it was about. It helped to finally figure out the truth. I don't think most parents realize that little kids are super-sensitive even though they might not really understand anything about what's going on. Like Chipper, the time I was little and painted him green. He didn't know he was green because dogs are color-blind too, but he knew something was wrong, and for that whole month of being green he slunk around all mopey and ashamed.

The déjà vu feeling wasn't just in my head, I decided. I was guessing my mom had found something — lipstick on my dad's collar or whatever — and they'd had a "talk," and that was why she'd started drinking wine and let me drive to the airport by myself and why they'd been acting civil mostly for my benefit while my dad tried to get Elwin Carl Dandridge off on a technicality. I ran up to my room and closed the door, but I was still in the same house with them so I went back downstairs where my dad was in his study on his laptop and my mom was furiously chopping celery. I grabbed the keys to Mom's Camry.

"I'm going for a ride," I said.

She stared at me openmouthed, but she didn't say a word. Five minutes later I was on the freeway in rush hour traffic, pretending to be a commuter.

I am not an idiot. I knew I was "acting out," as my mother would put it. "Acting like a brat" is probably more accurate. And I knew even as I was doing it that I was doing it because I was pissed at both of my parents and because taking my mom's car made me feel as if I had some control over things that of course I could do nothing whatsoever about.

I also figured that I'd pay some sort of price, because taking my mom's car was not the sort of thing responsible parents could overlook, so to make the most of it I ran around town listening to the radio until the gas gauge was lit up on empty, then drove home and left the car sitting inconveniently in the middle of the driveway. It was almost eleven at night by that time. The light in my parents' bedroom was on, but that was it. No porch light or anything. I let myself in through the side door.

The house was deathly quiet. I had a sudden and horrible fantasy of my mother shooting my father and then killing herself — the thought came and went in a flash, leaving behind a faint sensation of nausea. I sat down in the kitchen and waited for my stomach to settle. A minute or so later I heard a faint murmuring coming from upstairs. I couldn't understand any words, but I recognized the sound of my mother's voice, so I crept up the carpeted stairs and stood outside the bedroom door. Definitely my mother talking. My dad wasn't saying anything. I could hear parts of what she was saying: "He said he frud ammin . . ." *(silence)* "No! I don't think so, but last week — no, it was the week before I sobel greshat . . . force cure rattle . . ."

I sat down with my back to the wall and pressed my ear to the crack.

". . . lived with the man a long time, Beck."

She was on the phone, talking to her friend Becca.

I wondered where my dad was.

"He *says* he still loves me but he *would* say that — I mean, Beck, he's a goddamn lawyer for Christ's sake! The bullshit that comes out of his mouth!"

I'd never *ever* heard my mom talk like that.

"I know, I know, Beck, but I'm not going to jump before I know where I'm standing. Christ, I wish you were here. I need a martini."

I listened to my mother's profane bitching for about ten more minutes, learning nothing other than that all men are scum. I wondered if she was ever going to mention the astonishing fact that her underage and unlicensed daughter had driven off that very evening in the family car, but it never came up.

My dad, it turned out, was asleep on the sofa in his study.

The next morning, everything was eerily normal. My mother made breakfast and my dad asked me how I had slept — he always asked me that in the morning, and I always said "fine." Nobody said a word about me taking the car the night before. I thought that was kind of odd, but then I figured out that they were each afraid that if they brought up my car thing, we would have to talk, and if we really started talking, we'd end up talking about why Dad slept on the sofa and what was going on with them. None of us wanted that.

My parents must have had one of their "civilized" conversations, because the next night they slept in the same bed and for a few days we lived like perfect people in a perfect house where nothing bad had ever happened. I imagine their conversation went something like this:

"I hate and despise you for your philandering, dear, but I think we should wait for Kelleigh to get out of high school before we tear each other apart in divorce court."

"I agree absolutely, sweetie pie! That will give me time to enjoy a good deal of illicit sexual activity during Kelleigh's happy high school years."

"That's lovely, honeybunch, so long as you promise to be discreet, and so long as you do not attempt to conceal your assets in some offshore bank account."

"I promise, lovemuffin, so long as I can count on you not to tear my testicles out by their roots during our time together in court!"

Or something like that.

What bothered me most was how happy my dad seemed. He had a guilty rapist to defend, an affair to finance, and quite possibly a divorce to engineer. He was buzzing with purpose and holy zeal, a man on a mission. I got all that not from anything he said but just from watching the way he held his mouth and the crispness of his motions even at the breakfast table, and the way he talked on his phone, very terse and efficient, as if his every second was incredibly valuable. I sensed that his happiness — my dad's version of happiness, which was kind of the same as *purposefulness*, if that's a word — was all about having something important to do.

Two days later I called Deke. He was in a foul mood. His guy at the Mercedes dealership wouldn't give him his five hundred dollars back and wouldn't sell him another key.

"He says he's got to cool it for a couple months. Anyway, it makes no difference to *you*."

"It doesn't?"

"Yeah. You said you didn't want to do it anymore."

"No I didn't."

"I thought you did."

"I said I wasn't sure."

"That's what people say when they mean no."

"Not this people."

He didn't say anything.

I said, "So you can't get another key?"

"I didn't say that. You busy tonight?"

I told my mom I was having dinner at Jen's, then had Deke pick me up at the Cub Foods near my house. He showed up twenty minutes late, wearing his standard uniform: T-shirt, ripped jeans, and motorcycle boots. I was dressed in my usual nun chic: gray blouse with black pants. Very much the odd couple. Not that I thought it was a date or anything.

Deke was in a talkative mood. In fact, he wouldn't shut up, but most of what he said was pretty interesting.

"Most guys who steal cars are after those crappy 'C' cars: Camrys, Corollas, Cieras, Civics, Caravans," he said. "Cars that sell in the millions. They like 'em five or ten years old, 'cause that's when they start to fall apart, so there's a bigger demand for parts. Plus those older cars are easy to boost. No security systems or anything. A guy who knows what he's doing can pop the door with a slim jim, get inside, and hotwire 'em in like thirty seconds.

"Anyways, they sell these crappy cars to a chop shop, where they get broken up and sold for parts. You know that junkyard up on Washington Avenue?"

I didn't.

"Major chop shop. But there's not much money in it for the guys doing the boosting. Guy steals a Honda and sells it to a chop shop for a quick hundred bucks cash, then goes and spends it on dope. Me, I cater to the classier side of the business, the Benzes and Beamers and such. Cars like that don't get chopped. They go to Canada, Mexico, South America.

Neal takes orders from all over, mostly from dealers who can give 'em a new VIN and hide 'em in a boat full of legitimate vehicles."

I was fascinated by the way he'd slipped into using three- and four-syllable words, like "legitimate vehicles," and by how different it was from listening to Will.

We were in Deke's pickup, driving east on Highway 36. It seemed weird to me that a guy who specialized in stealing high-end luxury cars would drive a junky old pickup, so I asked him about that.

"Camouflage," he said. "Also, my parole officer would wonder how I could afford a nice car on my two-hundred-dollar paycheck from Wing's Wild Wok."

"How about a motorcycle?" I imagined myself on the back of a motorcycle with Deke driving.

Deke shrugged. "Bikes scare me," he said. "I had a friend who got killed."

We were driving toward Stillwater, a town west of St. Paul on the St. Croix River. Danny, Deke's backup key guy, worked at a restaurant in Stillwater called La Bellevue, a super-pricey French place. Danny was a valet.

Fancy restaurants, Deke told me, are a great place to score car keys, because a lot of supposedly smart rich people who spend big bucks on their food and their rides are stupid enough to hand their car keys to a valet, giving him the opportunity to go through the glove compartment and get information like the VIN number, the name and address of the owner, and the dealership where the car was purchased. Sometimes even a spare key — which if you think about it is an *incredibly* stupid thing to leave inside your car. But a lot of people do it, according to Deke.

Danny was just one of five guys Deke had looking for an S550 key. "I made some good connections when I was in jail," Deke told me. "It was like going to crime school. I got a couple valets, a mechanic down at Walton Motors, a guy who works at this detailing shop, and the parts guy at Bolton Benz. Problem is, these S550s, there just aren't that many. They cost like a hundred grand each. It's not like there's one on every block, and half of 'em you just can't get to, 'cause they park 'em in garages or on ramps. Neal's getting pretty antsy. He must have a customer breathing down his neck. He says if we can deliver this thing tonight, and if it's clean, he'll sweeten the pot. Two thousand."

"A thousand each?" I asked.

"Minus the three bills I promised Danny for the key. But this time you gotta drive it all the way across town. Neal wants us to park it at the Byerly's in St. Louis Park."

"Why there?"

"No cameras, and it's easy for him to watch, you know, to make sure the cops don't stake it out like they did the other one. He's a little spooked these days. Also, Byerly's is open twenty-four seven, so nobody's going to notice another car sitting there overnight. That's the plan, anyways."

The road swooped to the left and down a long hill that ran along the St. Croix into Stillwater, an old river town full of touristy shops and restaurants. It reminded me of Taylors Falls, only about five times as big, with a lot of people on the sidewalks.

La Bellevue was on Main Street in the middle of town. Deke made a U-turn and pulled up in front of it. There were two guys dressed in khaki shorts and powder-blue polo shirts standing next to the VALET PARKING sign. One of them walked around the truck to Deke's side and leaned in the window.

"Sorry, dude, we don't park crappy old pickups."

Deke laughed. He reached into his pocket and pulled out a roll of twenties.

The valet let the key drop onto Deke's lap. It was just like the key I'd used for the other Mercedes.

"Oops," he said, then reached for the money.

Deke held the money out of reach. "You got an address for me, Danny?"

"Oh yeah." Danny handed him a folded sheet of paper.

Deke passed him the roll of bills.

"*Gracias, amigo,*" said Danny, who looked about as Mexican as lutefisk.

Deke handed me the key and the sheet of paper, then put the truck in gear.

"Hey!" Danny was back at the window. "There's only two hundred here!"

"You'll get it," Deke said. He popped the clutch and we were off. I heard Danny yell something not nice after us.

"He's not happy," I said.

Deke shrugged. "I'm a little short. I'll get the rest of his money to him, plus another fifty, once we get the car. He'll be ecstatic."

That's another example of how Deke talked — one minute he says *ain't*, then a few seconds later he uses a word like *ecstatic*.

The sheet of paper the valet had given us was a receipt from the Mercedes dealer. It listed the owner's name — John R. Anderson — his address, the car's VIN, and the sticker price: $89,770.00.

"Read me the address," Deke said.

I read him the address. It was in Oakdale.

"What's the plan?" I asked.

"Recon," he said.

John R. Anderson lived in a "gated" development called Forest Glen, only the gate wasn't real — it was permanently open. Anybody could drive in and out. The phony gate was just to let the residents know how special they were. Inside, Forest Glen was a tangle of curved intersecting streets lined with enormous houses on tiny landscaped lots — the sort of neighborhood where nobody leaves their car parked outside. Two teenagers in a scruffy pickup truck would be quickly noticed.

"This sucks," Deke said as we drove past John Anderson's house. "We're gonna have to park outside the gate tomorrow morning and wait for him to drive out, then follow him to work. Assuming he *goes* to work. And we can kiss that bonus goodbye. Neal is gonna be pissed."

"I have Pilates in the morning."

Deke smacked the steering wheel with his palm.

"It's okay," I said.

"No it's not. I hate this shit. I mean, I make more money per hour at Wing's Wok."

"Then why steal cars?"

He looked at me, and we both started laughing — and even as we were laughing, I was thinking that we were laughing for completely different reasons, but it didn't matter, because in that moment, we were both on the same side.

As we pulled out of Forest Glen, an idea hit me. I checked John Anderson's receipt and there it was — his phone number. Two of them, actually — a home number and a work number.

I took out my cell and dialed.

A woman answered.

"May I speak with John?" I said.

"I'm sorry, but he's not at home," the woman said. "May I take a message?"

"Do you know when he'll be home?"

"I'm not sure. He said he'd be working late."

I realized then that I hadn't blocked my number, and my name would be on her caller ID. I had to say something that wouldn't make her suspicious later.

I said, "He has a job? I thought he was still in school!"

The woman said, "Are you sure you're calling the right John Anderson?"

"Johnny Anderson? Goes to Kennedy High?"

The woman laughed. "Sorry, you have the wrong number." She hung up.

I dialed the other number on the receipt. It rang five times, then was picked up by an answering system.

"You have reached the voicemail of . . . John Anderson. To leave a message, press one now. To speak to an operator, press two."

I pressed two. A few seconds later a brisk, chirpy voice said, "CronoMed Industries!"

"Hi, could you give me your mailing address, please?"

The woman rattled off an address.

It was that time around sunset when it's not really dark but most of the drivers have their headlights on, and the low sun bounces off windows and chrome, and everybody's in a hurry — or at least it seems that way. Deke weaved in and out of the I-694 traffic in a confident way that made me want to get behind the wheel.

CronoMed Industries turned out to be a complex of three new-looking buildings just north of the loop in Fridley — one of those places you drive past and idly wonder what they do there and then forget all about it until the next time you drive by. The parking lot was huge, but at that time of day, there were only a couple dozen cars still there. Deke spotted the S550 almost immediately, parked way at the back of the lot. It was white but otherwise identical to the one we'd grabbed from Ridgedale.

"Looks like he doesn't want anybody parking right next to him and dinging his paint when they open their door," Deke said.

He parked a few rows away, close enough that we could read the license plate.

"Check the numbers," he said.

I looked at the license number on the receipt. "That's it," I said.

"Okay then." He was looking around.

"What are you doing?"

"Checking for security cameras. I don't see any. Shit. Here comes somebody."

A man was walking from the building entrance toward us. I thought he was going for the S550, but he stopped at an SUV, got in, and drove away.

"This is bad," Deke said. "It's better when the parking lot is full of cars. The way it is now, anybody coming out of the building will see us."

A feeling of extreme anxiety had grabbed hold of me. As if something was supposed to happen but it wasn't happening. The way you feel when you light a firecracker and throw it and the fuse burns down but it doesn't go off, but you know it might and the longer you wait the less likely it is to happen. But it still might. Or like when you call somebody and leave a message and expect them to call you back, but they don't.

"Maybe we should wait till tomorrow," Deke said. "We probably lose the bonus, but it'll be safer."

I wasn't thinking about the money. I was thinking about the sudden *whoof* to the gut that happens when you get into a Mercedes and close the door and the air pressure increases slightly and you are wrapped in sudden silence. I could see in my head, visualizing like in Pilates, the button that starts the car. I could almost feel its smooth surface under my thumb and that slight resistance just before it clicks and the engine thrums to life.

"You okay?" Deke asked.

I shouldered open the passenger door.

"Wait!" he said.

I didn't.

"Kelleigh, don't!"

There is this feeling I get sometimes. It's like my head expands and everything gets sharp and hard and close — but not in a bad way. It's a good feeling, a safe and purposeful feeling, a feeling of being firmly connected to reality. I usually get it only late at night in bed — the ceiling of my room looks like it's only inches from my eyes, and even in the dark I can see it in microscopic detail and I'm sure that if I lift my hand, I can press my palm flat against it, but I never try because if it isn't true I don't want to know. There is a sound too. A sound without sound, a silent sound, felt more than heard, a buzzing or humming, rising and falling, like the sound a fetus hears before it has ears, or the sound you hear when someone miles away quietly says your name over and over again and you know you've heard *something*, but really you haven't.

I had that feeling then as I walked across the parking lot toward the Mercedes. My heels hit the tarmac with perfect trip-hammer regularity, dragging Deke's voice behind me like an elastic tether. I tugged on the door, but it didn't open. Deke was still talking, but I wasn't listening. I tried pressing one of the buttons on the key and heard a click. This time it opened. I quickly got in and closed the door, snapping off the rubbery banner of sound that was Deke's voice. I was embraced by a cocoon of silence.

Except for the roar of my breathing and my heart in my ears.

The car smelled different — a man's cologne plus leather seats plus the sour reek of cigars. Anyone who could own such an expensive car and then stink it up like that deserved to have it stolen.

I reached for the start button — but it wasn't there. Instead, there was a thing like a fat key slot. I sat there staring at it for what seemed like forever. Then I remembered that when we'd stolen the first Mercedes, Deke had told me that the keyless thing was an option, which would explain why the door hadn't opened for me.

There was a nub sticking out of the end of the key. I shoved it into the slot and heard it click home.

The sound of Deke's car horn pierced my cocoon. I looked toward his truck. He was waving and pointing from behind the windshield. I looked where he was pointing. A man wearing a suit and carrying a briefcase was walking quickly toward me from the building entrance. The second I saw the guy coming, three things happened: The guy in the suit broke into a run, coming right at me. Deke took off in his pickup, his tires smoking. Suddenly the Mercedes' lights started flashing on and off and the car started going *whoop-whoop-whoop!*

Funny thing. Even with everything happening at once, deep inside I was dead calm. I figured out right away that the guy had hit the panic button on his own key, and I remember thinking, *I can get out of this car right now and walk away and probably nothing will happen. I will tell the man I noticed the car door was standing open and I got in just to see what it was like to sit in a Mercedes-Benz and he might believe me or he might not but either way he'll just let me go because otherwise it will be a hassle and it wouldn't be like I actually did anything wrong except just sit in his car for a few seconds.*

But if I do that, I'll be stuck here with no way to get home.

I twisted the key. The siren stopped whooping. I put the car in gear and stomped on the gas pedal. The car leapt forward. I cranked the wheel to the right, trying to get around the guy, but he dived onto the hood and swung his briefcase against the windshield. It hit so hard I could feel the shock right through the steering wheel, but the glass didn't break. I twisted the wheel left, then right again, the whole time with the accelerator on the floor. He had the fingers of one hand locked on the edge of the hood by the windshield. With the other hand he swung the briefcase again; I ducked and flinched, but the glass held.

Don't ever let anybody tell you that Mercedes-Benz doesn't make quality windshields.

I had the wheel cranked all the way to the left, and my foot on the floor. The car was screeching around in a donut and the guy was looking right at me through the windshield, our eyes locked, then he went flying off, practically tearing off one of the windshield wipers, and I felt a thump from the back end, as if the wheels had bumped over a log. I straightened the wheel and headed for the exit, the wiper blade sticking out like a crooked antenna. *Don't look!* I said to myself, but I couldn't help it. I stopped and looked back. The man was getting up. He started toward me again, limping. His briefcase was crushed and the contents were scattered across the parking lot.

I drove off and did not look back again.

Later, trying to sort out what had happened, I remembered things in little bits and pieces. Like the way I'd felt when I realized I'd hit something and I was thinking it was him, not his briefcase. Either way, what I felt then — not knowing what had really happened — was not the horror of having caused injury to another human being but anger and frustration that he had gotten in my way, that he had tried to interfere.

I was also pissed at Deke for taking off.

Many car thieves are into speed and meth because they like the way it gets them all revved up inside, and they steal cars so they can buy drugs because just stealing cars isn't enough of a buzz for some people.

I did not drive directly to the Byerly's parking lot. Instead, I called Will. The second he answered, I said, "Meet me outside. At the curb. Fifteen minutes."

I didn't give him time to say no.

In a way I was going back on my promise to Jen that we would both break up with Will, but in another way I wasn't, because all I wanted to do was go for a ride with him. I knew it was a show-offy thing. I didn't care. I felt like I could do anything I wanted to do and whatever happened didn't matter because I'd done this thing, this car thing, like jumping off a cliff, and I'd survived. So from then on it was all free. I'd almost drowned in the Hummer, and I'd almost gotten pulled over by the police when I'd taken the Cadillac, and I'd taken my mom's car for a ride and nothing had happened, and I'd survived an all-out attack by a crazy briefcase man, so why not take my possibly-gay possibly-ex boyfriend for a spin in my new stolen Mercedes? I know it doesn't make sense now, but it did at the time.

Will was standing out in front of his house, all slouchy in knee-length shorts and a tank top. I think he'd grown an inch or two since the last time I'd seen him, even though it had only been two weeks.

I pulled over and rolled down the window.

"Hey," I said.

Will peered into the car and looked around like he was expecting somebody else.

"Hey," he said.

"Hop in."

Will ran his tongue over his lips. He made no move to open the door.

"Come on." I leaned over and pushed open the passenger door. Will stepped back. I said, "Are you getting in or what?"

"I don't know," he said. "Whose car is this?"

"It belongs to a guy named Johnson. Or Anderson. I don't know. Get in."

"Did you steal it?"

"Yes. Get in."

He shook his head and backed away a few more steps.

I put the gearshift in park, got out, and walked around the car. Will looked nervous. No, more like scared.

"Kelleigh . . . ," he said, holding up his hands, palms facing me.

I stopped a few feet away from him.

"Alton Wright is right," I said. "You *are* gay. Totally, totally gay."

Will lowered his hands slowly and the nervousness was replaced by an injured, angry look.

"I'm not gay," he said.

"Yeah, *right*." I put enough sarcasm into that last word to melt flesh. He just shrugged it off.

"If I was gay, I'd tell you," he said. "My uncle is gay, you know. It's no big deal. But I'm not."

The way he said it made me feel like an utter and complete bitch, which just made me madder. "I don't mean *gay* gay," I said. "I mean gay like chickenshit."

"That's not what you meant," he said. "You think I'm gay. Jen told me."

"Jen is full of shit too."

"Anyway, I'm not."

I opened my mouth to reply, but nothing came out. Suddenly our fight seemed like the most ridiculous conversation two people had ever had — *ever*.

"This is stupid," I said. "Come on, let's go for a ride."

"I don't get you," Will said.

"Obviously." I looked back at the Mercedes, its engine running quiet as a sigh. "I don't get you either."

"Look, I talked to Jen. She said —"

"If you want to talk, get in the car," I said.

Will looked up and down the street. I walked back around the car and got behind the wheel. I sat there for almost an entire minute, then the passenger door opened and Will got in. He looked around at all the leather and gauges and buttons and knobs.

"What does a car like this cost?"

"Ninety thousand."

He whistled. That's a guy thing. They whistle when something costs a lot. I don't think they know they're doing it.

"What about Jen?" I asked.

Will had found the radio concealed behind a panel on the dash. He cycled through at least ten different kinds of music in about ten seconds. I hadn't even known it was there. "Wow. Satellite," he said. He looked up and frowned. "What happened to the windshield wiper?"

"The guy I stole it from bent it." I put the car in gear and rolled away from the curb. Will was acting all nervous again, looking back at his house like I was kidnapping him. The car was beeping.

"Put your seat belt on," I said.

Will put his seat belt on. The beeping stopped.

"What about Jen?" I asked again.

"She . . . she said you thought I was gay because I didn't want to make out with you." He was pressing buttons on his door, making his seat go back and forth. "And she had this thing about, you know, that you guys were going to both marry me at the same time, except if I was gay, then we'd all have to move to a state that had gay marriage or something. It was really stupid but . . . I don't know. I'm not gay. I'm just not into you guys that way."

I was driving without thinking about where I was going, just making turns at the corners and stopping at all the stop signs.

"I mean, I really like you and Jen for, like, *friends*. But I guess you're just not my type."

"What's your type?" I heard myself ask.

Will shrugged. "I don't know. Like Phoebe Line."

I almost drove up onto the curb. "Phoebe *Line*?"

"Yeah."

Phoebe Line was an *elf*. She was about four foot nine with a pointy nose and a squeaky little voice and this long almost white hair that hung all the way down to her miniature ass. In high heels she would maybe come up to Will's armpit. All of which would have been okay except that her physical stature was matched by her mental stature. In my opinion.

"Have you ever *talked* to Phoebe Line?"

"Sure," Will said.

Phoebe *Line*?

"She's nice," he said.

I turned right, then turned right again.

"Where are we going?" he asked.

I told him I was taking him home.

"Whatever," he said.

The funny thing about Deke was that even though he was a car thief/ex-con/pothead with no future, he was at least a guy who had an agenda I could count on and understand. He knew what he wanted. Money. He would be pissed at me for making him wait at Byerly's. That was okay with me. At least he wasn't all squishy and "whatever" and "Phoebe Line is so cool" like Will.

I parked in the middle of the Byerly's parking lot, between a panel truck and a minivan, put the key on top of the left front wheel, and went into the store. I was suddenly starving, and Byerly's is a great place to be if you're hungry — they have a huge deli section with everything from fried wontons to sushi to chocolate croissants. I bought an egg roll and a bottle of pomegranate juice, then went back outside to sit on one of the benches and wait for Deke. Assuming he hadn't already given up on me — otherwise I'd have a long walk home. I was finishing my last sip of juice when Deke pulled up to the curb. I motioned to him to wait, walked over to the other side of the entrance, and put the egg roll tray in the trash and the empty bottle in the recycling — doing my bit to save the planet.

As I got into the pickup, Deke said, "What happened to you?"

"Nothing."

"I been driving in circles for almost an hour." He slammed the truck into gear and popped the clutch; my head snapped back against the headrest.

"I had to run some errands," I said.

"You're lucky you didn't get cracked!" He banged the steering wheel with his fist. "How d'you know that Benz doesn't have a locator in it?"

"Because if it did, the guy would have just called the cops. He wouldn't have jumped on the hood and tried to smash through his own windshield with his briefcase."

"Bull*shit*!" Deke banged on the wheel again, then forced himself to calm down and said, his voice level, "He might have if he was mad enough. That was messed *up*, what you did. And stupid. If he got my license number, I'm screwed. I am so screwed!"

"He wasn't looking at you. He was looking at me. What's the matter with you, anyway?"

"Now he can ID you!"

I looked at his eyes. His pupils were huge, like big black holes. It hit me then what was going on.

"You're *high*," I said. I didn't know if it was weed or meth or what, but it was *something*. I expected him to deny it but he didn't.

"What're you, my parole officer?"

"Pull over," I said.

"What for?"

"Let me out. *Now!*"

For about three seconds he just kept on driving, jaw pulsing, hands squeezing the wheel so hard I thought he'd crack it. He jerked the wheel to the right and hit the brake and bumped up onto the curb and stopped.

"Get out!" he said. Like it was his idea.

After I watched Deke lurch off in his pickup, I walked back to Byerly's, grabbed the key from on top of the front wheel, got in, and drove the Mercedes home. I parked on the street a few houses away and listened to the radio for a while. It was only about eleven o'clock. I wanted to make sure my parents were asleep before I let myself in, because I didn't think I could stand all the pretending. I was listening to some head-banger rock — not what I usually listen to, but it felt right — when a bright light hit the side of my face. I shaded my eyes and squinted into it. A police car had pulled up alongside me.

I had thought my heartbeat had maxed out before when that guy had jumped on the hood, but that was nothing compared to the banging that was going on in my chest right then.

I rolled down the window. The cop lowered the light slightly so I could see her.

"Is everything okay?" she asked in a way that could have meant absolutely anything from *I want to help* to *You are going to jail*.

"Fine," I said, smiling even though my voice sounded to me like a squeaky robot voice. "I'm just waiting for my brother." I don't know where *that* came from.

"Do you live around here?"

"I live in Wayzata," I said, naming a random outer suburb. "My brother was supposed to stay over with his friend Adam." I gestured at the Garbers' house, just across the street. The Garbers had no children; I hoped the cop didn't know that. "But then he got sick so my dad asked me to come pick him up." The lie formed itself effortlessly. "I think he's just homesick. He's only seven."

For the next several seconds, the only sound was my heart whooshing blood through my arteries. I could see the cop making her decision: Was it worth asking for my license? Was it worth running the license plate? Didn't she have better things to do?

I said, "He had one little backpack and I've been sitting here ten minutes waiting for him to find all his junk." I laughed. "You know how little kids are." The cop nodded and gave me a short smile as the blood roared in my ears like, *goosha, goosha, goosha*. I had this really weird thought then — two thoughts, actually. One was that the veins in my eyeballs were about to explode. The second was that if she would arrest me, maybe my heart would slow down.

"You take care," she said, and drove off. The back of her trunk had NEIGHBORHOOD SERVICES printed across it. She hadn't even been a real cop, just one of those community cops who do things like put up barricades for block parties and check on old people to make sure they're not dead. My heartbeat slowed, to be replaced by a creeping nausea that crawled up the inside of my spine and spread like tendrils through my belly. I sat there for a few minutes, waiting for the nausea to subside, then put the car in gear and drove back to Byerly's.

It took me almost an hour to walk home. I passed a lot of parked cars and checked to see if maybe one of them had the keys in the ignition, but none of them did. The good thing was that when I finally got home the house was dark and my parents were asleep, so I didn't have to deal with them. I was a little surprised though that at least one of them hadn't stayed up to wait for me.

The next morning I told my mom I was having major cramps and couldn't do Pilates. I stayed in my room the whole day, going back and forth between *Moby-Dick* and watching car theft videos online. Some of the videos were guys filming themselves stealing a car and then posting it on YouTube, which has got to be the stupidest thing imaginable next to chasing a giant albino whale that wants to kill you. I must have watched fifty videos of car thieves in action, mostly hot-wirers and carjackers. The funny thing was, I felt nothing in common with any of them. I actually had more in common with the whale.

I had gotten almost all the way through *Moby-Dick*, chapter one hundred thirty, and Ahab was still chasing the white whale. I might have finished it right then, but I heard my mom making cooking noises and I was getting hungry, so I went downstairs. The kitchen smelled like garlic and cigarettes. She was seeding and peeling tomatoes. Most people would just open a jar of Ragú, but Mom didn't do anything the easy way — not even spaghetti.

"How are you feeling?" she asked.

"Better. Did you know that a car gets stolen in this country every twenty-eight seconds?"

"I didn't know that."

"I just read it online. I thought it was interesting."

"It's frightening," she said.

"So Dad's not coming home for dinner?"

She paused before replying. "That's right," she said. "How did you know?"

"It smells like cigarettes in here."

She dropped a few more tomatoes into the pot of water and stirred them around for a few seconds, then lifted them out one at a time with a slotted spoon and put them into a colander.

I said, "Usually you smoke out on the porch and throw your butts behind the rosebushes. Unless Dad's out of town or something."

"He had to fly back to Colorado."

"To talk to the car thief again?"

"Yes!" She slammed the spoon onto the counter, then pretended like she'd accidentally dropped it.

"Are you and Dad going to get divorced?"

That set her back. But instead of saying no, she said, "Whatever gave you that idea?" Then she said, "I don't want to hear it." She slipped the skins off three more tomatoes, chopped them, and added them to the ones already simmering on the stove.

"I don't care if you smoke," I said.

I didn't hear from Deke that day. No surprise there. I didn't even care about the money, but it bothered me that he didn't at least call to tell me if Neal had gotten the car okay. Just for, you know, a sense of closure.

Speaking of closure, I finished *Moby-Dick* that night. The last five chapters were pretty good, or at least a relief, because finally the whale showed up and did his thing and almost everybody got killed.

The next morning, I wrote a review and posted it on the school library website. There were a bunch of other reviews up, including a review of *Speak* that Jen had written. (I happened to know she had already read it last year, but, as Will would say, *whatever*.) Alton Wright had posted a long review of *Of Mice and Men* that I would bet anything was written by his girlfriend, Tracie. Nobody else had read *Moby-Dick* or any other book as old and long and complicated, so I figured I'd get extra points or something for that, even though my review was kind of critical of whaling in general. It was funny that about ten seconds after I posted my review, Deke called. I saw it was him from the caller ID, so I let it go to voicemail. Then I waited a few minutes before listening to the message.

"Hey, crazy girl," he said. "You in jail, jailbait? I guess not or you wouldn't be getting this. Listen, I got some cheese for ya. Pizza with extra cheese. Yum. You know where to find me. Lunch break's at two. See ya."

My mom had Book Club again, so I offered to drive her, and of course, being ever-eager for mother-daughter bonding opportunities, she said that would be nice. "We're meeting at

Francine's this month," she said. "She always puts out a nice spread. I bet she'll have those little fruit cups."

I ran upstairs to change. I put on a clean pair of pants and a long-sleeved cotton blouse that I'd picked up on sale at The Gap.

"You look nice," my mom said, giving her head a critical tilt.

"What's wrong?" I asked.

"Nothing." She laughed. "My black-and-gray daughter. I guess I should be thankful you're not running around in nothing but a tube top and a thong."

It was only a ten-minute drive to Francine Abrams's house, but on the way there, Mom managed to tell me that Dad had called and he was coming home and everything was okay in Colorado. From which I inferred that they'd had some other sort of conversation entirely, and they weren't going to get divorced after all.

She also told me she was quitting smoking for real on her fortieth birthday which was in September, and that I should never start smoking, and that she was planning to make individual chicken potpies for dinner.

"I already made the crust and the filling," she said, lighting a cigarette. "I just have to put them together and throw them in the oven."

"Wow," I said.

"It's easy," she said.

"I mean, wow, you're actually smoking in front of me."

She cracked her window and expelled a lungful of smoke. "You're old enough to see that your parents are not perfect."

I laughed. I was going for a friendly chuckle, but it came out sarcastic.

She looked at me sharply. "Wait till you have a daughter of your own, then you can judge me."

"I'm not having children." I meant it.

My mother laughed a laugh just as dry and sarcastic as my laugh had been.

"Sweetie," she said, "you have no idea."

"Neither do you."

She shook her head and blew more smoke out the window.

When we got to Francine Abrams's house, I told my mother I wanted to sit in the car and listen to music, and that's what I did for a while. I saw her look out the window at me twice. I waited until a full five minutes went by without her peering out at me, then I started the car and drove to the mall.

Deke Moffet was sitting in the food court, sucking on a giant soda, tapping his right foot, and glancing around with little jerks of his head. He looked straight at me twice before he recognized me. He started to stand, but froze halfway up and sat back down. I walked over and stood across the table from him. He stared at me, hollow-eyed, jaw pulsing, and sucked down a few more ounces of soda. He shrugged, looked away, scratched himself behind his ear, looked back at me and said, "Every time I look at you, I freak out. Little Miss Perfect Kelleigh Monahan, car thief."

"I'm a retired car thief."

He muttered something, but because he had the straw back in his mouth I couldn't make it out.

"I stole a couple cars," I said. "But it's not who I am. There's a difference."

"Not if you get caught, which you will, if you keep doing shit like you did yesterday."

"It was the day before yesterday."

He looked away. "Whatever." He reached into his back pocket and pulled out a wad of bills. "Here."

I took the money and put it in my purse without counting it.

He said, "Neal knocked off a couple hundred for the wiper blade and the dents on the hood. He's a prick."

"Whatever."

Deke looked over his shoulder toward Wing's Wild Wok. "I hate this job," he said.

"So quit."

"I can't. Parole violation."

I turned away.

"Wait a second!"

I turned back.

"Neal needs an Escalade."

"Call Marshall."

"Marshall's messed up. Dude hasn't slept in like two weeks." I wondered how long it had been since Deke had slept. "Listen, I can get a key," he said. "I can get a key tomorrow, I think. The vehicle's a demo just sitting waiting at Prestige over on 394 and I know one of the salesmen there. Same deal. We grab it and drop it at Byerly's. Piece a cake." His knee was going up and down so fast his whole body was shaking.

"I have to go," I said.

"Wait!"

I kept on walking.

I think the main reason I was attracted to Deke was because my expectations were so low to begin with that I figured he couldn't possibly disappoint me. On a professional-car-thief level, that is. But it didn't work out that way.

Sooner or later everybody turns out to be a disappointment.

Two weeks later, on my sixteenth birthday, Dad and I went to the DMV in his Lexus so I could take my road test. On the way there he told me that Elwin Carl Dandridge had been released for lack of evidence. The DNA collected from two of the women he had allegedly raped turned out to be contaminated, and there was some question about the chain of custody — the way my dad explained it, it looked as if the investigators had pulled some "funny business."

"These guys try so hard sometimes to make an airtight case, they just can't resist cheating a little," he said.

"You mean they knew the guy was a rapist, so they made up evidence to put him away? Is that bad?"

"Actually, they had some pretty solid evidence in two of the cases, and they figured if two cases were good, three would be better. So they duplicated it. If Dandridge had been forced to rely on a public defender, he'd still be in jail."

I loaded my mouth with sarcasm and said, "Wow. Good *job*, Dad."

He laughed.

He *laughed*.

I wanted desperately to shake him, but I knew if I went after him for his ethics he'd just want to argue me out of it, and being a professional arguer he was really good at that. So I said, "You know, if you and Mom want to get divorced, it's okay with me."

That wiped the smile off his face.

"Why would you think we want to get divorced?"

"Because you're having an affair and Mom hates you."

He looked over at me and I saw his face take on that blank, serious, sincere look that he used in court.

"*That* is simply not true," he said.

"Which part?"

He pulled into the parking lot and focused all his attention on finding the perfect parking space. Once we were parked he said, "Kelleigh, I don't know what you think you've seen or heard, but you are misinterpreting it."

"Like that DNA evidence?"

"That's right."

He said that with a straight face.

I aced the road test.

I took Will and Jen out for a ride in my mom's Camry — my first legal road trip. We went to Wagner's Drive-In for burgers and malts. Will didn't have any money, of course, and all Jen had was her mom's credit card, so I paid out of my car theft money.

Looking at the wad of cash I pulled out, Jen said, "Birthday money?"

"I stole a car and sold it," I said.

They were both sort of quiet.

"Just kidding," I said. Then, to change the subject, I asked Will how his romance with Phoebe Line was going, which took Jen by surprise.

"Phoebe Line?" she asked.

Will shrugged. "I just said I thought she was nice."

"She *is* nice," said Jen after a moment.

I didn't say anything. I felt like I was a thousand miles away, alone, driving through mountains and desert, and Will and Jen were nothing but hologram projections out of my past.

Three days before school started, I was at Ridgedale all by myself, looking for a new sweater in black or gray, but mostly thinking about my dad and my mom and Jen and Will and Deke and Jim Vail and Elwin Carl Dandridge, and they were all tumbling through my head like clothes in a dryer. Then I saw the guy whose Nissan Jen and I had taken a couple of months earlier. He was walking through Macy's with his briefcase. I remembered then that I still had his keys in the bottom of my purse. I wondered if he'd had his car re-keyed. The more I thought about it, the more curious I got, so I went out to the parking lot and walked up and down the rows of cars until I found it.

The key fit.

I got in the car and closed the door. It wasn't as quiet inside as a Mercedes, but still, it was comforting to be sealed up in there. I could hear the thrumming in my head again, the sound of blood rushing in my ears. I started the car and pulled out of the parking space. The car had a full tank of gas, which was good even though I had no place I had to be, but that was okay, because at least I felt like I was going somewhere.

I think that a lot of car thieves just like to steal cars and drive. Also, they think they will never get caught even though most of them eventually do and they know it but they just don't care.
